SAVING

TOM

BLACK

SAVING TOM BLACK-

A JAKE SILVER ADVENTURE

JERE D. JAMES

MOONLIGHT MESA
ASSOCIATES

SAVING TOM BLACK

Printed in the United States of America

Published by:

Moonlight Mesa Associates, Inc.
18620 Moonlight Mesa Rd.
Wickenburg, AZ. 85390

www.moonlightmesaassociates.com

ISBN: 978-0-9827585-6-4

LCCN: 2009929137

Introduction

The Erie Railroad train left from New York on a cold, dirty gray March morning in 1888 on just another routine run. The last passengers of this inauspicious journey would disembark from the Kansas Pacific Railroad in Topeka, Kansas, several train changes later. The trip and its destination posed nothing unusual except for the forty-four, wide-eyed, pale little passengers huddled tightly together, each with an identification tag pinned to the front of their ratty coats and jackets. The group was yet another batch of orphans destined for the Midwest, destined for a better life - or at least a different one.

Orphan trains, the popular term used for these human cargo carriers, had been increasingly common since the mid 1850s when local New York City reformer, Charles Loring Brace, adopted the growing, popular notion that homeless, destitute, vagrant, even criminal children would be better served in the fresh air and wholesome environment of the West. Given the grim alternative that many of these children faced, the brighter future each might find in the West certainly seemed more promising than the dreadfulness faced on the streets of New York City, where most of the children lived and worked. While many had been placed in orphanages by parents too poor to care for them, some had simply been abandoned to fend for themselves.

Trains transported thousands of these children to the yet unpopulated West, to be placed for adoption or, in some instances, for indenture. Males were generally the preferred sex, since many shorthanded farmers needed boys to work the fields. Females were shipped west also, but in smaller numbers. Many girls ended up being "taken in" and trained as household helpers and servants, and on occasion, even wives.

Of the forty-four children transported this day, seventeen of the younger children would be adopted upon first being put on display at local churches and halls; ten boys would be taken in primarily for their ability to perform farm duties; four boys would be secured by families running a business and would ultimately learn a trade; two boys would run off and head farther west in search of a life of adventure; three would run away and return to New York City; three of the older girls would be put to work as domestic help; four of the girls would be given to prospective husbands, and one girl would disappear. The fact that all the young passengers could not be accounted for would not be recognized until after the train had made its last stop and the accompanying adult supervisors had begun their return trip to New York.

Orphan Train Escape

"WHERE in the devil could she have disappeared to?" The speaker, a thin, nervous woman spoke in hushed tones to her associate, the anxiety and anger in her voice unmistakable. "Should we even say anything? Really, I don't think we should make a statement at all. I'm not even certain what train we were on when I last saw the girl. Perhaps it was the last one, the Kansas Pacific."

"Mrs. Hawkins, we must report this incident." Joseph Longman, a supervisor for the Children's Agency replied in a voice filled with remorse and self-castigation. "We would be most derelict in our responsibilities by not saying anything. I'm sure the girl has come to no harm, but really, we must inform the authorities as soon as possible."

"I fear that will cast a most dubious light on our proceedings," the woman huffed. "We have an excellent record of child placement, Mr.

Longman. I do not wish to do anything to jeopardize the fine work that our director has done thus far. This incident could cause a scandal. You know, there are those who would like to stop our efforts."

Both sat in silence as the train rumbled on in the growing twilight.

"There's another issue, Mr. Longman, which I hesitate to bring up, but fear I must."

"Yes?" Joseph Longman looked up, alarmed at the prospect of hearing more bad news from the overbearing woman sitting across from him.

"I can't say for certain, but indeed I almost positively *can* say that the girl stole forty-four dollars from my valise. I'm more than certain when I think about it. I distinctly remember her saying she would watch my things while I dealt with the younger children who were crying and raising a fuss. This was when you were dealing with that one ruffian and several other squabbling older boys. Of course, I didn't check the contents of my bag when I returned to my seat. I would never suspect any child of having the audacity to steal the very money needed to feed the children! Yet, the more I ponder the more I simply know that the missing girl is nothing but a juvenile criminal. A thief, pure and simple."

"Mrs. Hawkins! Forty-four dollars? I… I… I'm speechless. Are you quite certain you haven't misplaced it?"

"It's gone, Mr. Longman. I've emptied my bag and inspected the contents half a dozen times."

"Oh, my. I wonder if we shouldn't file a report with the local law enforcement authorities."

"That would evoke even more cause for scandal. Already there are those who accuse us of transporting only juvenile delinquents and criminal offenders. We cannot give our naysayers any more reason to think so. No. I say we simply forget about the little thief and go on as though nothing has happened. That way we save ourselves from embarrassment and further scandal."

Longman didn't respond, thinking instead of the blonde-haired, angelic looking girl. Reclusive and silent, she'd said nothing during the trip. He'd assumed that she'd been preoccupied, contemplating the change she was old enough to know was coming her way. The children were usually never told where they were going and why, but the older ones often knew anyway. Sometimes letters from siblings who'd been transported earlier came to the orphanage, although the program tried to keep siblings united. Rarely, however, were siblings adopted by the same family, and occasionally they were sent west on separate trains, as had happened in this instance.

"The fact that she took her small bag tells me she simply ran off and was not abducted. You know as well as I that many of these girls are incorrigible and beyond salvation, having had untold manner of sinful experiences living on the streets." Mrs. Hawkins lifted her chin, arched her eyebrow, and peered down her long, beaked nose at her companion. "You know to what I refer, of course," she said disdainfully, her beady brown eyes boring into Longman's.

"Yes. Sadly, that's true. But she certainly didn't look…" Longman trailed off.

"Looks, dear sir, are often deceiving. I don't need to tell you that. You've been in this business long enough to know that a sweet young girl often has the heart of a harlot. Forgive me for so saying."

"Forty-four dollars? You're quite certain?"

"Absolutely. She's a thief and a ne'er-do-well. I think we should forget her. I will just fill out forms saying that she was taken in by a family. The Smiths. That's a common enough name."

"But what if someone from the agency checks? They do home visits."

"Mr. Longman, you worry needlessly. It is impossible to keep up with these children. Everyone knows that. Let me handle this. You just go about your business and forget we've had this conversation. I should never have brought it up in the first place."

"Very well. If you insist." Longman stared at the darkening landscape, knowing Mrs. Hawkins was right. No one would discover the disappearance of one child. No, not a child, really. Her paperwork listed her age as sixteen, but often the ages of the orphans were guesswork, and sometimes even altered to facilitate placement. For all he knew, the girl could have been anywhere from twelve to twenty. No, not twenty. Possibly as old as seventeen or eighteen, though.

He handed the missing girl's paperwork to the harsh figure sitting across from him. Glancing one last time at the name on the documents, he said a silent prayer that the girl would acknowledge the error of her ways and repent. *Oh, Lord, be merciful to Elizabeth DuBonnet. Bring her to salvation and to safety, but let her suffer mightily for her transgressions.*

"You know, we transported her mother and older sister just last year, or maybe the year before," Mrs. Hawkins said. "There have been so many; I can't keep track of them all. They're all the same, really. Downtrodden. Uneducated. Impoverished. Only capable of bearing children, it seems. She's probably run off to join one of them."

"Really? I had no idea!" Longman responded in surprise.

"Indeed. They were sent as brides. Both lost their jobs as seamstresses due to one of the modern factories opening. That's when they first came to the agency for aid. I believe I recall that one went to a Mormon. I don't remember about the other. I was quite surprised that the director would agree to the Mormon arrangement. I know nothing about Mormons, really. I just know from Mr. Collins that the girl's mother and sister were sent west a year or so ago, during that terrible time when so many of the working poor lost their positions. We couldn't keep adults at the orphanage, so we placed them where they could be of good use as productive members of society."

"Would there be a record of where they went? If so, that might be how we can trace the girl," Longman spoke hopefully.

"Who knows where they went, Mr. Longman. They were sent to one place, but odds are they left for another with the new husband. It would be impossible to trace the Mormon bride, in any event. Now please, we've agreed that we are going to let Elizabeth DuBonnet go and not mention her again."

"Of course. You're right. I'll not say another word. But how will you account for the missing money, Mrs. Hawkins? Forty-four dollars is a most substantial sum to lose."

"I will come up with something, Mr. Longman. It is my duty, and I will take full responsibility." She sat musing for a moment, anger clearly continuing to build, then said, "Perhaps a wire to the local sheriff in Topeka might be a good idea after all. I must think on this. I need not mention that the girl is missing or a runaway, simply that she is a criminal, a liar, and a harlot."

The Atchison, Topeka and Santa Fe

IT happened quickly. Elizabeth, nicknamed Betsy, DuBonnet didn't know if she had the courage, but suddenly she found herself swinging down a handrail and dropping from the train just as it began to pull away from the depot. Not daring to turn around to watch the train make tracks, she ripped the name tag branding her an orphan from the threadbare coat she'd been issued, picked up her small travel case, and tried to walk with a casual step down the boardwalk. With a heart still beating heavily, afraid to believe her incredible fortune, she quickly crossed to the shadows cast by an awning, lest either departing adult espy her. Had she actually made it? She experienced a delicious rush of giddiness over her sudden, newfound freedom, and she deeply relished her first moments away from the beady eyes and dour glares of Mrs. Hawkins and the soulful, lingering looks of Mr. Longman. So far her ploy had worked perfectly, and she knew she would be safe, at least until the train arrived at its next stop. How long would that be? Being cautious, she didn't dally. She had a plan that had been long in the making, and she must continue its execution at once.

It took no time to find a mercantile shop in the busy frontier town of Topeka, Kansas. Trying to appear confident, as though she shopped every day of her life, Betsy boldly entered Millman's Mercantile, where she encountered the curious stares of several customers clearly unaccustomed to seeing an unbonneted female, let alone one whose long hair, secured by a simple clasp, hung unadorned down her back. Unaware of her singularly unstylish yet arresting appearance, she brushed past the furtive patrons, reminding herself that no one knew anything about her, and that she had no reason to blush. As far as anyone was concerned, she had every right to be shopping on this fine day.

"May I help you, miss?" the sales clerk quickly approached and asked.

"I need a hat, if you please," Betsy answered as she thought a prim and proper young lady might.

"Yes, so I see. Well, you are in luck because we have a lovely selection of ladies' hats over this way. Some of these exquisite millenary creations are just recently arrived from the East and are exact replications of the style now worn in European capitals," the sales clerk announced loudly, for the obvious benefit of any shoppers within hearing who might also decide to buy one.

"No. I need more of a man's hat," Betsy casually responded. "It's for my brother's birthday."

"Oh, my. Do you know the size?"

"I'm sure if it fits me, it'll fit him," she quickly responded. "We're twins," she added, smiling merrily, pleased with the clever, impulsive explanation that almost caused her to laugh outright.

She tried on several for effect, but bought the cheapest available, a black sombrero style with a higher crown and slightly broader brim than most, deciding it would be good for tucking her hair into. She could also pull it low over her brow to hide her face.

"Good choice," a tall man dressed in a tailored, black suit commented as she handed the hat to the waiting clerk.

"Thank you," she mumbled, alarmed, avoiding eye contact and quickly turning away. Something about the man caused her anxiety level to soar. His regal bearing intimidated her, and his eyes seemed to peer through her. Could he be a *real* western sheriff, or an outlaw even, like the ones she'd read about in the dime readers? Her heart began to beat rapidly as she remembered the forty-four dollars in the small coin purse pilfered only a short while ago. She walked slowly down an aisle, trying to nonchalantly browse while surreptitiously watching the man in black depart after he cast another glance in her direction. Relief and a rebounding of her good spirits did not return with his exit, however. "I must be more careful," she reprimanded herself.

Two purchases later, Betsy left the shop. Only after she cautiously looked about and didn't see a lawman, did her confidence and composure slowly begin to return, along with the growing certainty that her plan would work. She still had thirty-four dollars left, having spent ten dollars on a hat, jacket, and a pair of ready-made boy's boots. All that remained to buy was a horse, which she planned to do at her final stop. She prayed that she could buy a decent mount and still have money left for travel needs.

Uncertain how much time remained before she'd be discovered missing, she began her hunt for a west-bound train, wanting to make it at least as far as the Arizona border. She'd seen a map and knew the border might be as close as she would get to the town where her mother now lived.

It had been her sister's letter that had galvanized her to take these drastic measures. Margaret had written a teary missive, lamenting her deplorable life, expressing extreme dislike of her Mormon spouse and the other wives. She'd threatened to kill herself if someone didn't help her. It was typical of Maggie to be dramatic, but the tone of the letter was so hysterical and desperate that it prompted Betsy to take action, instead of waiting for her mother to send for her as she'd promised.

Taller than average, with large sky-blue eyes, a delicate nose set in an oval face, an abundance of blonde hair, and a painfully undernourished body, Elizabeth DuBonnet might have been royalty in another time, another place. Here she felt the full weight of her mother's and sister's woes on her thin shoulders. It wasn't just their misery, though, that wore her out. She often succumbed to a profound sadness when she remembered bits of the idyllic childhood she'd lost when her mother dragged her sister and her to New York City, insisting a better life awaited them there.

Having been born and reared on the remains of a plantation destroyed during a great war, like any child she hadn't understood the extent of the ruin and disrepair. Betsy never saw the vast, weed-choked, scorched fields surrounding the dilapidated mansion, the sunny yards that once held flowers, ponds and meandering paths grown tall with weeds. She saw only her dolls and mud pies sitting by the scum-coated ponds, her pony in a distant field, her mother busy entertaining gentlemen somewhere in the empty rooms. She often wondered what happened to the pony. Thinking of the abandoned animal starving or being shot by poachers brought tears which she quickly blinked away. "This is a day to be happy," she reminded herself. "Not a day for tears!"

Stealing the money from Mrs. Hawkins had been her one regret. Betsy knew the funds were intended to feed the children on the trip, yet they'd been given nothing but mustard sandwiches for days, causing the little ones to cry and the older ones to complain and become troublesome. She'd waited to take the money until the very last, intuitively knowing that Mrs. Hawkins would never use the funds for the children's food. The despicable woman would pocket it instead. Waiting until the last possible moment almost assuaged Betsy's guilt.

She felt no guilt that she'd stolen two pair of pants, two shirts, and extra socks from the laundry facility at the orphanage. Having only a small valise, she'd been forced to wear some of the items under her dress. Once she discarded the ugly, oft mended, gray muslin dress and thin-soled shoes, she'd be ready to start life over – once again.

But first, the train. Should she buy a ticket and spend more of her pilferings, or just find a place to hide aboard the carrier? She knew the answer before the question fully formed.

She stood for a moment in the cool, spring air, shivering slightly as a pale sun tried to peek through thinning clouds. Deep down she sensed that this was a world where a new life, a truly good life, might await her. Despite her urgency to find her sister and mother, more than anything Betsy simply sought a life of peace. To ask for happiness seemed greedy. She just wanted tranquility, and if she allowed her dreams to run truly rampant, she pictured herself alone in a field of flowers, safe and secure. Maybe snowcapped mountains would surround her hidden valley. Would it be too much to ask for a small cabin, a garden, and a creek nearby? Now she knew she was being silly and wistful, but it was fun to dream. She'd wiled away hundreds of hours at the orphanage fantasizing a life far from the crowds and filth of New York, far from the austere, cold dormitories and hallways of the friendless orphanage, away from ruffian boys and crying children, everybody cranky, tired, and pasty white as a wan moon. Now she stood alone in this unknown frontier world, vacillating between shock at what she'd just done, fear of what would come next, and amazement that she'd so far succeeded.

She stepped into the street. "I can do this," she resolutely muttered, feeling the warmth of the emerging sun. "I can do this, and I *will* do this."

With determination she turned to find the tracks of the Atchison, Topeka and Santa Fe Railway. The railway to her dreams.

***

"You take good care of this horse now," Jake Silver said as he handed the lead line to the attending porter inside the train car that would transport his horse and a few other livestock.

"Yes, suh. Don't you worry none about this fine animal, suh. Old Thomas'll take good care of him."

"I'm much obliged," Silver said as he handed the man whose name tag read Thomas Jefferson a half dollar.

"You're always welcome to come back and visit your horse at any stop, suh. Anytime," Thomas Jefferson responded, carefully tucking the silver piece in his pocket.

"Thanks. Maybe I will." Silver nodded, stepped from the car, and headed to the passenger compartments.

He knew he was being watched as he strode along, and he also knew, without being vain, that he cut an imposing figure. Six foot one, two hundred five pounds and heavily muscled, the new Arizona U.S. Deputy Marshal walked with assurance, certain in the knowledge that he would now be the most important and powerful lawman in the Arizona territory. Even now he was one of the highest ranking lawmen in the entire area. He wore his newly tailored three-piece suit and handmade boots with pride. A new black, flat-crowned Stetson covered his sandy hair, casting shade over his hazel eyes. His physique and movements showed him to be a man of speed and enviable athleticism. He exuded both intelligence and danger, irresistible to women because of his intense independence and general indifference to their wiles, and a profound peril and mortal danger to any man who might consider crossing him.

"How long until we get to Prescott?" he asked a passing porter.

"That depends on the tracks and the weather, sir. This time of year there can still be snow at the higher elevations in New Mexico, and track vandalism of course. Some comforts can be found in the dining car if you're in need. And of course you may disembark and dine at any of the stops."

He sat, looking out at the busy Topeka street. It had been a long journey from Texas, where he'd been born and reared. The trail had finally led him to the practice of law in these new territories. He hoped this new career would satisfy his need for adventure and travel more than driving cattle had, which he'd done for a passel of years. He'd enjoyed life on the trail, seeing the beauty of the country, and he thoroughly enjoyed meeting head-on the unexpected, unlike his fellow drovers. Nothing like a good stampede or river crossing to add some interest to the trip. Unlike most cattlemen, Silver was an excellent swimmer and harbored no fear of drowning. He relished being the first to ford a river, and he always assumed the point position in guiding cattle across. The monotony, though, of endless days watching cattle mosey along at a snail's pace had finally gotten to him. He'd quit even though he'd been offered the job of trail boss. He liked the independence he'd felt as a trail hand. Literally, he could leave at any time. Might leave without his pay, but he could leave. As a trail boss, he'd be honor bound to deliver the herd. Jake Silver was a man of his word.

After reading an ad describing the newly posted marshal's job, he quickly warmed to the idea. He'd be his own boss in his own territory, more or less, and the new Arizona territory at that. His expert knowledge of Spanish and his quick and deadly draw had been significant factors in landing him the job, even though he'd had far less law enforcement experience than other applicants. Fact was, he'd only been a posse member half a dozen times in Texas for long-haired Marshal Jim Courtright, but the man's recommendation had served him well. A few years as a deputy under Singer, Tilghman, and Bell in Dodge City, as well as their glowing references, had sealed the deal. He had a well- established reputation as a fast draw, but also as someone who resorted to force as a last measure.

He wondered if he'd ever see Texas again. Sometimes he hoped not. After his father returned from the war minus a leg, life on the ranch turned bitter and sorrowful. Even though only a toddler when his father came home after fighting for the Rebs, Jake could sense despair and trouble. The homestead his father and grandfather had painstakingly built and groomed into a working ranch, fell into disrepair. There'd been barely enough money for his oldest brother and sister to attend college, but now his brother was a successful banker in Fort Worth who helped advise and invest the funds that the ranch generated. His sister had taken up teaching school, having spent many childhood years practicing on him. His three other brothers eventually agreed to keep the homestead a working ranch and poured their energy successfully, after several years of near bankruptcy, into cattle and horses. Jake, ten years the youngest boy, found himself at odds with a ranching future. Too young to join the Texas Rangers at fifteen, he'd joined a cattle drive two years later, promising his mother it would just be for one trip. After five years on the trail, he'd earned a reputation as being one of the best in the business. He was smart, tough, and knew no fear.

The train began to lurch forward, and Jake Silver settled in his seat, setting his saddle and bag of weapons next to him. He allowed no one to touch or stow these items. Certain that everything was secured, he tipped his hat low over his eyes and dozed off.

Stowaway

"WHAT you doin' hidin' on this train, young - -" Thomas Jefferson halted. Was the young person before him a girl or a boy? Dressed like a boy. Did it look like a boy?

"You come out from behind there right now."

The person - - a girl? - - slowly stood, brushing straw and debris from her jacket.

"I'm gonna hafta report you to the author'ties," Jefferson began, not quite certain who the correct authority might be.

"Please, don't report me. I'll...I'll give you a dollar if you don't tell."

"A whole dollar? Lemme see."

The girl pulled a silver coin from her pocket and handed it over.

Thomas Jefferson took the coin and paused, turning it over and over in his fingers. "My my. Lucky day for ol' Jefferson. Got me a half dollar earlier. Gonna make my whole month's wages this week alone if this keeps up." He smiled, pocketing the coin and looking the stowaway over carefully, still not certain of the sex of the person he was facing.

"What's yer name?" He paused for an answer, and when none was forthcoming he asked, "What're you doin' on this train?"

"Going west. I'll get off when I get there, I promise."

Jefferson chuckled. "Guess you will, all right. That's the end o' the line, sonny." He turned and proceeded to muck out the horse's stall. "Never told me yer name."

"My name is…John," a small voice answered haltingly.

Jefferson peered closely at the scrawny stowaway. "Don't look like no John I ever seen."

"Well, just call me John. I'll just sit here and cause you no trouble. I don't want to cause trouble."

"Whatcha goin' west for? Dat a long way from home for ya, ain't it? You runnin' away?" Jefferson again peered closely at the stowaway while he proceeded with his chores.

"No, I'm looking for my mother and my sister."

He chuckled. Despite the passenger's obvious efforts not to be, the stowaway was drawn into the conversation.

"My mother's living in a mining camp near a town called Wickenburg. Have you been there?"

"Wickenburg? Can't say as I have. Heard of it, though." He stopped, hands on the pitchfork, and looked long and hard at the young critter before him. He could now see long wisps of hair trailing from under the hat. A nose far too pretty to be a boy's and a face too fair convinced him that his passenger was not named John.

"Why don't you tell me your real name, young lady. Maybe I can help ya out. You're headin' for big trouble goin' where you are. Hate to see that happen to a purty little girl like you. Pardon my liberties if I offend," he said, bowing ever so slightly.

"It's no offense, Mr.- -"

"Name's Thomas Jefferson," he said as he set the pitchfork in the corner and motioned with his gnarled fingers for Betsy to come out further from behind the bales of hay.

"Thomas Jefferson? Like President Thomas Jefferson?"

"The one and only. My great granddaddy was a slave for President Jefferson. We all been named Thomas Jefferson ever since." He paused, widening his eyes for effect. "So, what's your real name?"

"Elizabeth DuBonnet. I'm called Betsy. You can call me Betsy, if you please."

"DuBonnet. My. That's the purtiest name I ever heard. What kinda name's that?"

"It's French. Don't know what it means. But my mother said she was born in France, so that makes me French, too. I guess it does, anyway."

"DuBonnet," repeated Jefferson, letting the name roll off his tongue. "My my. DuBonnet. Lovely name. Much nicer than Jefferson."

"You can use it on yourself if you like. I don't mind," Betsy volunteered.

Jefferson knew the gesture was a cloaked bribe to allow her to remain aboard the train.

"Thomas DuBonnet. I do believe that has a nice ring to it. Makes me sound like someone I'm not."

"Sure. Go ahead. You can be Thomas DuBonnet all you want. Tell people you're French."

"I believe I will, Miss Betsy. I'd like to have a different history than what I got."

"I need a name, too. Maybe you can help me pick one that sounds just right for me. I need a boy's name."

Jefferson looked at her carefully. "Why you wantin' to be a boy, Miss?"

"I've got to find my mother and sister. I figure it's safer to travel in these parts as a male," she said, hesitating. "You know what I'm meaning, don't you?"

"Yes, Miss, I'm 'feerd I do." Jefferson paused, looking thoughtfully at his young passenger. "But yer never gonna pass for a boy lookin' like that."

"Like what?"

"With all that purty blonde hair peeking outta yer hat, for starters."

"But what can I do? I've just got to find them. I've got to. They're *depending* on me. They *need* me," Betsy whined, an unmistakable pleading in her voice.

Jefferson sat in silence thinking for some time, arms crossed, his eyes traveling from the pathetic looking figure before him to the floor, and back again. He had become fully aware of his predicament. He'd never before been alone in a room with a white woman, nor had he ever talked to one so openly either, both being hanging offenses where he'd come from, war or no war. Why should he help her? But, why shouldn't he help her? She was breaking all the rules of convention, too, even more so than he was by passing herself off as a male.

"Let me think on it a bit," he finally answered, running his large, crooked hand through his graying hair. "Got no experience in this area. Gotta think."

"Well, didn't you ever help other people escape? I read about it happening," Betsy said in an encouraging tone.

"I heard about them folks. I wasn't part of it. I value my neck too much, I 'spect," he said as he stood, taking the pitchfork and flinging horse manure out the train door. "You best sit back in that corner again. Case someone wanders back here to check on things."

Betsy settled in the corner and watched Thomas Jefferson, now Thomas DuBonnet, muck out the horse stall.

"That's a nice looking horse. Who's it belong to?"

"Some gentleman dressed up all in black. Looks like a lawman to me. Got that look about 'im. Nice enough. Give me a half dollar to keep an eye on it."

"I'd sure like to get myself a horse like that."

"Don't get no ideas about horse thievin'. That's a hangin' crime out here. You already broke enough laws, I reckon."

"I wouldn't steal a horse," Betsy quickly responded. "I was just wishin' out loud. I've got to get myself a horse when I get out to Arizona, though. You know where I can buy one? How much do they cost, anyway? When will we be in Arizona? I'm almost out of money."

"Land sakes. You goin' all out, I can see that." Jefferson smiled as he threw out the last pile of manure.

"Well, do you know?"

"How much you got?" he asked.

"Not very much. And I need a saddle and stuff to go with it."

"Lordy. Lordy. Lordy." Jefferson stood, gazing out the train door as he slowly shook his head. What he was hearing baffled him.

"Well, first off, we a long way from Arizona. We still be in New Mexico for now."

"We are?"

"Albuquerque comin' up in a bit. It's a big enough town so's you can get a horse there, and from what I understand, the best place to buy in Albuquerque is from the Mexican's stable. I guess you could get a decent mount for maybe ten dollars. Maybe. If you can pay more you'll get a better'n."

"Ten dollars? Truly?"

"It won't be much of a horse, Miss. An' it pro'bly won't include a saddle and all that horse ridin' stuff folks call tack. Can't rightly say. Never bought a horse before."

"It's the Mexican place?" Betsy asked.

"Yeah. Sure. Right in town. Can't miss it. It's just down a bit from the depot."

"Okay. So, have you thought of a name for me?"

"Jus' let me think on this for a bit. My head's spinin', I'll tell you that much."

"Who you talking to?" a voice suddenly asked from the door.

Jefferson quickly looked over and saw Betsy duck behind the hay bales.

"Talkin' to no one, suh."

"Saw your lips moving when I came up to the door," Jake Silver said.

"Jus' prayin', suh. Jus' prayin'."

The man appeared satisfied with Jefferson's answer and turned his attention to the horse. "How's he doing back here?"

Oh, he ridin' mighty nice, suh. The train don't seem to bother him none t'all."

"Good. Good to see his stall clean, too. You're a good man. I thank you."

"Not at all, suh. My pleasure."

Silver now stood by the bales behind which Betsy hid. To keep his nerves at bay, Jefferson kept his eyes downcast and slowly walked to the far end of the car as though inspecting all the animals, desperately hoping the visitor would leave quickly.

"Beautiful country." Silver moved toward the open train door. "Mind if I slide this shut? It's a mite breezy on the horse. Don't want him catching cold. You got enough light in here with that window, don't you?"

"Certainly, suh."

"Well, I guess I'll wander on outside and look around, then, since everything seems okay here. What's the name of this stop?"

"This here be Layton, just outside Las Vegas, New Mexico, suh. We be stopped here mebbe ten minutes more – at most. Then on to Albuquerque. Come by anytime, suh."

The imposing man nodded and sauntered off.

"Don't you dare show yer head right now," Jefferson said to the hiding girl as he crossed himself, trying to look righteous should the man look back. "That was too close. We gotta figure somethin' out here fast."

"I know," Betsy volunteered from her hiding place. "I've been thinking you can cut my hair. That way, if that man comes back and finds me he'll just think I'm a boy getting a free ride."

"That might work," Jefferson responded. "I got no better ideas." He paused a moment. "You sure you want that purty hair all cut off?"

"Sure," Betsy responded, sounding not in the least certain.

"Well, we best do it before he returns. He most likely won't come on back here real soon since he was just here, but I got a feelin' he'll be checkin' his horse agin at some other stop. His kind takes good care of their horses. They takes better care of their horses than some men take care of their womenfolk. You stay there. I'll fetch my knife on over."

"Knife? You don't have any scissors?"

He heard alarm in her voice. "Got no scissors, but I'm right good with a knife. You c'n trust me, Miss Betsy."

"You've got to stop calling me Betsy. I need a name, Thomas."

"Well, since I'm usin' your'n. Whyn't you use mine?"

"Thomas Jefferson?"

"No, just use Thomas. Shorten it to Tom."

"That's good. I like that. What about a last name?" Betsy removed her hat. Her hair tumbled down like an avalanche.

"I heard about a Tom Black one time. You got a black hat. Just go with Tom Black. Easy to r'member that way."

"That's perfect. I'm Tom Black. Don't forget. Stop calling me Miss Betsy."

"Okay, Tom Black," he said. "Come here and let Thomas DuBonnet give you a haircut. This 'bout the craziest thing I ever done."

Still he hesitated. Never had he touched a white woman's hair before, and the softness and color held him in a trance as he slowly let the long blonde strands sift through his gnarled, black fingers. Upon such close inspection, the color was unlike anything he'd ever seen. White and gold strands so intermixed as to blend to a most astounding yellow. The texture was silky and fine, yet the hair hung thick and heavy.

"Well? What're you waiting for?"

"Just admiring your beautiful locks, Miss...Tom, I mean."

He took the knife and, gathering the hair at the nape of her neck, sawed through the golden strands. He held the hair up to the light momentarily, taking one long, last look before discarding it. "If you don't mind, I'd like to keep a few strands, Miss…Tom, I mean. I never seen or touched hair like this before."

"Help yourself, Mr. DuBonnet. I'm not using it now."

As the train moved along, he continued to carefully whittle away the remainder of her hair, attempting to fashion it much like a man's shaggy haircut. "Let me take a good look," he said finally.

They both stood, and he walked slowly around her. "Put your hat back on."

She complied. "How do I look?"

"Much better – as far as being a boy is concerned. I think you might pass now. Here. Put a little hay dust on your face. Pull the hat down like this." He paused and looked critically at his creation.

In truth, she still could not pass as a boy if someone looked at her closely, but she'd be okay if a person only glanced. "You look just like a Tom Black should look," Jefferson finally said, trying to calm her growing uneasiness. The haircut was about the worst he'd ever seen. "You'll do just fine if you c'n lower your voice a bit. Keep your eyes down. Don't look nobody in the eyes. They see those blue eyes you got and they gonna get curious and maybe look at you closer."

"Thanks, Thomas. I don't know how I can repay you for your help."

"Oh, we all need a little help from time t' time. Maybe someday you be helpin' me. Ya never know," he replied, now beginning again to realize the enormity of what he had just done. He'd been alone with a white woman, talked with a white woman, and now he'd touched a white woman. Men like him were shot for far less – sometimes shot for no reason at all.

"Can I ask just one more favor?" Betsy asked.

"Try lowerin' yer voice and askin' agin."

"Can I ask one more favor?"

"That's better, but you gotta work on lowerin' that voice."

"Could you help me buy a horse? I've ridden a horse before, but I've never bought one. I don't know what to look for or how to begin."

"Miss Betsy - -"

"Thomas, my name is Tom Black! Please address me as such."

"Tom, I've already got myself into a peck o' trouble if I ever get found out. I don't think I can go any further."

"No one will know, Thomas. You have my word. If we get stopped, I'll just tell them I tricked you."

"Mebbe. We'll see. You get some rest. You got food?"

She shook her head. "I'm almost out of money. I didn't know it was so far to Arizona."

He sighed but stifled a groan. She was becoming more trouble than he needed. He knew now he should have turned her over to the porter when he'd first found her. "Here, you can eat some o' my molasses and bread I got over here." He handed her a small sack which contained his lunch. "Now get some rest. Yer gonna need it."

She smiled in gratitude and he could readily see she'd never be taken for a boy if she ever flashed that smile at anybody. Only a woman could smile so sweetly. "Stop yer smilin' and eat, and don't smile no more, neither."

He furtively watched her eat, then settle down. Soon her eyes closed, and he could see darkening circles beneath them. Runnin' away was hard work – he'd done it himself. He wondered about her – where she came from, how she came to be in a livestock car, where she was going, and what would become of her. Life in the West was not meant for a beautiful, young girl such as herself to be wandering about alone and unprotected. He shook his head sorrowfully, fearing the worst. "Lord, bless this little lady and keep her in Your protection," he prayed quietly. He wasn't much into prayer, but felt it couldn't hurt under the circumstances.

He took a sampling of hewn hair now strewn in the hay and kicked the remaining clump about. Tying a string around one end of the bundle, he secured it and carefully tucked his golden prize into an inner coat pocket. He'd always remember her this way, no matter what fate befell her.

What the hell. He'd help her buy a horse and then he vowed to be through with her. Through, before he got into even deeper trouble than he'd ever been in before. The train would lay over in Albuquerque, at least through the dinner hour, depending on the schedule. Sometimes it stopped overnight. Either way, there'd be time enough to assist Mr. Tom Black however he could.

Albuquerque

"THANK you, suh. Thomas Jefferson DuBonnet surely does 'preciate your generosity. You departin' here, suh?"

Jake Silver handed Thomas Jefferson, apparently surnamed DuBonnet, a silver dollar when he returned to the livestock car to fetch his horse.

"Think so. Can't stand this sittin' around staring out the window. I'm not due in Prescott for a month yet. Thought I'd take some time and see the territory."

"Yes, suh. Did I hear you be the new U.S. Deputy Marshal?"

"Thomas Jefferson DuBonnet," Silver mused, bypassing the question. "Interesting name for a…" Silver paused. He started to say darky, but stopped himself. He had to remember he was no longer in Texas. Northern Arizona was antislavery. "Interesting name for a man of your ancestry."

"Yes, suh. My grandfather come from France. He worked for a king. The king of France, in fact. The very one."

"Did he now. That's mighty interesting." Silver turned away and rolled his eyes as he began to lead the horse to the exit. He noticed a tuft of long blond hair in the straw. Picking it up, he could tell by the texture that the strands weren't from a horse's tail. "Where'd these come from? This is human hair."

Thomas' eyes opened widely, in a shocked, alarmed manner. Then the old man seemed to recover his wits. "Can't say as I rightly know, suh. Must have come in with the hay, I reckon." Silver handed the strands to the black man's outstretched hand.

"Very odd, don't you think?" Something about the hair tugged at Jake, but unable to quickly recall the memory, he let the matter go.

"Yes, suh. Mighty odd," Jefferson said, giving the strands a cursory glance then casting them back into the hay without another thought.

"All right. I thank you again, Mr. DuBonnet. I'm much obliged for your service."

"Good day to you, suh."

Silver nodded, leading his mount down the ramp. The horse, excited and nervous, raised a momentary fuss but settled after a few snorts, wild-eyed looks, and whinnies. The animal, nearly sixteen hands, was his pride and joy. Part quarter horse and part Arab, the animal showed a quarter horse's sturdiness and speed, but had the endurance of the desert-bred Arab. He'd paid 300 dollars for the animal in Kansas City after a lucky night at the card tables, spent considerable time training the animal, and had since been offered a thousand dollars for it - - which he'd scoffed at.

The horse clearly needed exercising. The animal had traveled a lot of miles standing in a train car, and now it moved about nervously, ears pricked to attention. Silver fitted the blanket and saddle, loaded his weapons into their respective scabbards, strapped on his holsters, and mounted.

Turning about, he flagged a porter. Flipping him a silver dollar, he commanded more than asked, "Would you mind taking these to the hotel for me? Tell the clerk I'll be there shortly. The name's Silver. Marshal Jake Silver."

More than happy to oblige, the porter scurried off. A silver dollar was perhaps a full day's wage for the man. Jake harbored no concern about the safety of his goods. You got what you paid for, and he had a tendency to be generous to a fault.

With that, he clucked quietly and the horse began to move down the street in a smooth, extended trot. At the edge of the small town he opened the animal to a lope for a few miles, finally advancing into a gallop. Within moments the horse settled into a long, stretching run, and horse and man moved as one. Five miles later Jake brought the horse down to a lope, then a trot. Circling about, he maintained this pace back to town. The two would have many long rides ahead of them. No sense risking a stone bruise or sore muscle from running all out after so many days of idleness.

"You got a lot of miles ahead of you, Buddy. No point in overdoing it the first day."

It was approaching early evening when he re-entered town. Dismounting in front of the Mexican's stable, Jake tied the horse and walked through the loafing shed-like structure to a back corral, looking for the owner. He stopped in the shade of a doorway, watching the curious assembly gathered. He recognized Thomas DuBonnet instantly, but not the young, scrawny kid at his side. He assumed the Mexican now speaking was the owner of the Mexico Stables.

"You got ten dollars, meester?" The Mexican asked in a heavy accent. "Ten dollars buy thees horse."

The boy looked to DuBonnet for guidance, then the black man spoke. "Now, Poncho, you know you got other horses for ten bucks. The boy's got a long way to ride. He needs a better mount than this old nag."

"Thees a ten-dollar nag, then."

The boy said something to DuBonnet and the old man paused for a moment, then asked, "What you got for twenty dollars?"

"Twenty dollars buy that nice gelding there," the Mexican answered, pointing to a silver-colored grullo on the far side of the corral. "Good horse. Good feet. But young. Young horse go fast. Leev long time," he quickly added.

DuBonnet and the boy looked the horse over, but Jake could see that neither really knew what to look for. "Maybe I can help," he said, stepping from the shadow of the doorway.

DuBonnet nervously cleared his throat and the boy stood still as a statue.

"So, you looking for a horse for yourself, Mr. DuBonnet?"

"No, suh. Just helpin' young Tom Black here get hisself a horse. He got a long ride, and this here Mexican bandit wants twenty dollars for that there gelding."

"Nice looking animal," Jake commented. "How old you say he is?"

"Maybe *tres anos. Possiblemente quatro*," the Mexican answered nervously, reverting to Spanish, now that a knowledgeable, daunting man was present.

"Nah. This horse is barely three, I'd say. Maybe two still. Good animal, though. How much training he had?" Jake looked the young quarter horse over. A grullo well over fifteen hands, the horse was not yet fully developed, but the animal showed excellent lines, strong legs, and good feet, still unshod.

"*No se.*"

"You don't know? Maybe the horse is only worth ten dollars if it's that green and not well trained. Never been shod, either. The horse'll need shoes if it's going any distance. What do you think?"

"*Si*. Ten dollars. Ten dollars good, *bueno*?"

"Tom here needs a saddle, too," DuBonnet spoke up in an obvious endeavor to take advantage of the man's presence.

"Saddle ees more. Saddle ees ten more dollars," the Mexican said defiantly. His tone indicated there would be no negotiating.

DuBonnet conferred quietly with the boy. "Tom here says that's okay if you throw in a saddle blanket, reins, and the rest of the gear."

The Mexican started to argue but, after casting one glance at Silver, changed his mind. "*Si*. You come tomorrow. Ready here. Pay now."

Again the two conferred. "Tom says he'll pay when he comes tomorrow."

"Wise decision," Jake injected. "Maybe young Tom there ought to try the horse out first. Make sure the horse is manageable. What do you think?"

The Mexican looked dismayed, but DuBonnet nodded approvingly.

"For now, *amigo*," Jake interrupted, "I need to board my horse for the night. I'm going to rub him down, water and feed him myself. I'll be leaving tomorrow around noon. *Comprende*? You take good care of this horse." Jake tossed the man a silver dollar. There's another of these when I pick him up tomorrow. You take care of him, *comprende? Muy importante.*"

"*Si, senor,*" the Mexican answered, pocketing the coin and nodding respectfully. "You come tomorrow carly to ride thees horse," he said, returning to DuBonnet and Tom Black. "Breeng money."

"She uh – he'll be here," DuBonnet answered, clearing his throat.

Jake watched the black man and strange boy disappear through the building. Wondering about the odd pair, he walked the short distance to the hotel where the staff greeted him cordially.

"Marshal Tucker's been around looking for you, sir," the front desk clerk informed him. "He left a note. Said for you to come by at your convenience in the morning, if you would. I've taken the liberty of placing your valise in your room, sir."

"Much obliged." Jake nodded, taking his key and climbing the creaking stairs to the room. He hadn't realized how exhausted he was until he sat on the squeaky bed. "Sittin' around too damn much," he muttered to himself. He forced himself to his feet, neatly hung his coat, vest and shirt, and placed his hat on the bureau. Pulling his boots off, he massaged his feet until they totally relaxed. Lying back on the bed, he closed his eyes and dropped off to sleep instantly.

It seemed he had no sooner shut his eyes than daylight streamed through the curtained window. Looking out the tiny aperture, he could see that the train had already made tracks. The clear morning air seemed cool and breezy. He'd have to wear his heavy coat. Easier to wear it than to try to pack it with his gear. That'd leave room for the new suit he was so proud of.

He had a lot to do before he could leave. He wondered, as he looked out at the distant, snow-covered peaks, if he shouldn't have arrived from the south, maybe taken the train into Benson and then ridden north. He just hadn't wanted to go back through Fort Worth. If he'd gone through Texas he'd have felt compelled to check in at the ranch.

He'd lived in Kansas City for almost six months working as a deputy for Ben Shipp, when he received word that he'd been hired as a new U.S. Deputy Marshal for the northern Arizona territory. It just made sense to leave from Kansas to travel to Arizona, and not backtrack through Texas in order to catch the Southern Pacific.

Northern Arizona could be downright cold, he reminded himself. Might as well get used to it. He set about arranging his saddlebags to carry his suit and the extra pants and shirt he carried along in case he got wet from inclement weather. Traveling in wet clothes was a surefire way to kill a man, especially in the cold. He'd have to pick up a bedroll, utensils, and grub for the trip. Needed quite a bit of stuff, including more cartridges, now that he looked things over. Might not get out of town today after all. There was no rush, though. He wasn't expected in Prescott until late April or early May. Plenty of time to see the new country.

"Quite a big commotion down at the Mexican's stable early this mornin'," Silver heard a customer say as he entered the café. "Some young kid got bucked off that grullo of Poncho's coupla times. Finally broke down and started cryin' like a girl."

The group of men enjoyed a hearty laugh. Jake remembered the young Tom Black and his companion from the day before and figured the horse was as he'd said, pretty green. Green horse, green rider, always spelled trouble.

"Poncho finally got the kid mounted and the horse settled. Quite a show for awhile."

"Kid get hurt?" someone asked.

"Nah. You know boys. Seemed like a tough enough little critter. Kept gettin' back on, even with tears runnin' down his face. Skinny little guy. No paddin' to land on."

"Well, at least Poncho got rid of that wild thang. Hope the kid don't get kilt on it."

"You shoulda seen Poncho. He looked beat to hell and back just from shoein' the horse. I din't think he'd shoe that hell bastard horse for nobody."

"I don't like those grullos none. Think they're bad luck. Spooky, if you ask me. I'll take a good sorrel or roan any day," one of the men volunteered.

The talk rambled on to the weather and other local topics. Jake ate a hearty breakfast of bacon, eggs, and pancakes, chased down with two cups of black coffee, wondering what the story was on the boy. Probably a runaway who'd come west to catch the action, just like a thousand other youngsters from the East. For all he knew, the kid could be the next William Bonney.

After breakfast, Silver finally directed his steps to see the infamous Dan Tucker, retiring lawman of New Mexico, who was temporarily filling a spot in Albuquerque. It would be good to talk to the man and get the news on who the local gunslingers and outlaws were in the northern territory that he undoubtedly would eventually have to deal with. Tucker had a sterling reputation as a lawman, and Jake felt flattered to be meeting him. He'd heard often of Tucker's exploits, and knew him to be one of the fastest, most deadly guns in the West. Jake saw it as a hopeful sign that the man had lived long enough in his profession to retire. Jake wanted to do the same. As a former U.S. Deputy Marshal, Tucker would be able to offer sage advice.

On his way to Tucker's, he saw the boy whose name he'd heard was Tom Black coming out of the mercantile, staggering under a small load of gear: blanket, canteens, other trail items, and what looked like a small handgun. The handgun didn't bode well. He hated to see a youngster carry a gun. Seems like they all tried to use 'em on the wrong people. He'd carried a gun as a kid, but he'd been raised on a ranch, riding and shooting hundreds of prairie dogs with his father's military guns. He'd known how to handle a gun since he'd been seven years old. His expertise and dead aim had gotten him pretty regular work as a posse member for Jim Courtright.

He strolled across the street, all the while watching Black continuously drop and retrieve various items as the boy tried to arrange the gear more securely onto his newly acquired gelding. "Where you headin', son?" Jake asked, extending his hand in greeting to the youth.

"West," the young boy answered nervously, avoiding all eye contact while attempting to shake Silver's hand.

A small, almost delicate hand met Jake's large, calloused paw. He'd never felt such a revolting, weak grip come from a male. Despite himself, worry began to sprout in Jake's mind. The boy was obviously too young and too vulnerable to be on his own.

"West is a mighty big place. Anywhere in particular?" he asked, trying to study the lad closely. The kid's hat blocked most of his face, making it difficult for Jake to see much. Inexplicably, the hat troubled him.

"Nope. Just west," Tom Black answered, turning away, still failing to secure his blanket and other gear.

"Let me give you a hand with that," Jake said, taking pity on the lad. "You ever used a gun before?" he asked offhandedly.

Tom Black nodded yes, but Jake intuitively knew he was lying.

"Where's your folks, son?" Jake asked, as gently as he could.

"Mama's in Arizona. Goin' there now," the boy answered gruffly, then spit a tiny stream of sputum as he untied the horse and prepared to mount.

It quickly became clear that the horse was far too tall for Black to get a foot in the stirrup to pull himself up.

"Hold on a minute, son. Why don't you - -"

"Just get outta my way, mister. I got no time to talk."

Jake had to twist his mouth around to keep from laughing as the lad tried to mount the horse. The equine devil kept moving off. "Let me just give you a hand mounting. You might want to keep in mind that a good-sized rock or log will be a big help for mounting when you're alone out on the trail."

Despite a strong urge to stop the boy from leaving, Jake had no idea what he'd do with him if he did so. The West was filled with youngsters exactly like the one before him. Settling the horse,

Jake bent over and cupped his hands for the boy to step onto. Expecting more weight, he boosted the youth almost over the other side of the horse.

"I'm leaving later today. If you want to wait, I can ride with you until our paths separate. Might be safer traveling with someone rather than being out on the trail by yourself this time of year. There's still Indian trouble from time to time. Wild animals. It's a rugged country, son." Jake studied the boy's exposed mouth and chin and could tell he was wavering.

"No thanks." With that Tom Black took the reins and, holding onto the pommel, nudged the horse to move. After receiving several small, futile kicks, the animal began to mosey down the street, walking sideways a good deal of the distance.

Probably catch up with him at the edge of town if that's all the faster he's gonna move, Jake thought as he recrossed the street to meet Marshal Dan Tucker. But he also noted with satisfaction that the grullo was indeed a good looking animal.

On the Trail

BETSY breathed a sigh of relief as the settlement of Albuquerque faded from view after she'd ridden a short distance down the well-traveled road. If the route continued to be marked this clearly, she'd have no trouble getting to Wickenburg - - assuming she was heading in the right direction and this was the Beale Wagon Road. Doubt and worry clouded her every move and thought. Now that she was actually underway, she felt terrified. The easy part was over although, she reminded herself, when she'd taken on the first part of this adventure, those obstacles also had seemed insurmountable.

Her horse settled down, but she wasn't sure which of them was actually in charge. If the animal bolted, or bucked, and she fell off, she knew she'd be helpless to get it back. She repeated Thomas' advice: heels down, lean back, hang on.

It had been hard seeing Thomas Jefferson wave goodbye as the train pulled away. Ironically, when she'd lived in the South she'd never once talked to a black person. It was the biggest rule in the house, and the only one the master insisted the girls obey. Although curious about them, she largely grew to fear and distrust black people. Yet she instinctively trusted Thomas and had told him everything. He was the only friend she'd had in a long, long time. Indeed, she couldn't remember ever having a friend other than her sister. Thomas had even given her back her silver dollar before he left. "Here," he'd said. "I gota feelin' yer gonna need this mor'n me."

He'd sat with her late into the night outside the depot, answering her questions and giving what advice he could. "Remember, no eye contact. No smilin'. Keep your voice low. Don't talk to no one if you can help it. Don't never act scared. Actin' scared is what gets people into trouble. Folks in this part of the country consider scared a sure sign of weakness."

He also gave her a list of items to buy at the mercantile with her remaining money, including the handgun if she could afford it. "Don't try to shoot nobody with that, just use it to scare off any wildlife. Wave it around if you think you gotta, but be darned careful you don't pull it out when someone is wearin' six shooters, or yer gonna be left for coyote feed. Men in these parts shoot first and ask later. Spit now and then. That's what men do real reg'lar."

Maybe she should have waited and ridden with that man. He seemed nice enough, but even if her instincts hadn't told her he was a lawman, Thomas had said as much himself. She didn't want to be around a lawman, of all things. She supposed they'd circulated a wanted poster on her already. Besides, there was just something about him that made her...made her feel different. Something....

"Okay. I've made it this far. I can make it to Wickenburg. The hard part's over," she said aloud, struggling to bolster her flagging confidence.

Should she try to trot the horse and get there quicker? But what if he went faster than a trot? She'd ridden her pony quite well as a child, but she hadn't ridden in years, and she'd never been on such a large, wild animal before. Besides, her backside and left shoulder ached considerably from the falls she'd taken earlier that morning. "My behind's probably bruised because of you, horse," she muttered angrily. Perhaps she should change her tone in case the horse responded with more bucking because of her nastiness.

"You need a name, horse. We're going to be together for a long time...I hope. You got a name?" She patted the animal's neck. "So you're a grullo, whatever in the heck that is. I could call you Grullo. Do you like Grullo for a name?" She thought for a few minutes. "No, that's ugly. How about Moonlight? You look like the color of silver moonlight. I could call you Silver, maybe. Do you like Silver? No, I'm going to call you Moonlight." Immediately she began to feel more relaxed now that the horse had a name, as though a name meant he was tamed.

Where should she camp? She had no idea where the next town was. She had no map, she realized too late. What little confidence she'd garnered quickly plummeted, and it became all she could do to keep from turning back. At that moment she entertained her first good idea of the day.

To the left, boulders of every size lay scattered among the meager trees. She'd hide over there and wait until that man rode by, then she'd follow at a distance. With no other plan coming to mind, she nudged Moonlight to the mound of rocks several hundred feet from the trail, a perfect hiding spot with a few trees, brush, and large rocks spread around the area. Before she dismounted, however, she made certain something on which she could stand to mount again lay nearby.

Moonlight immediately began nibbling at wild bunch grass which kept her from lying down and stretching out her sore back and bottom. It was then that she realized she had no way of securing the animal, so she'd have to hold onto the reins while he munched away. Tired and cranky now, she didn't want to have to hold the horse. Why had she not thought of buying a rope? She was down to nine dollars after her purchase of the horse, saddle, and trail gear. How could she get all the way to Wickenburg if she could never lie down to sleep but had to hold the blasted animal every time she dismounted? Frustration caused tears, and anger came and went. No matter how hard she cried or stamped her feet, the problem remained. The thought of returning to Albuquerque loomed larger and seemed less undesirable now that she realized the mistakes she'd made. It was getting cold, too.

Suddenly Moonlight's ears pricked and the horse stood erect and tense. "Easy, boy. Easy Moonlight. Shh. Calm down, boy." Could she hold the horse if he decided to take off?

Peering from her hiding spot she saw a horse and rider loping down the trail. She recognized the horse from the train car and knew it had to be the same man who'd earlier tried to dissuade her from leaving alone. Quickly she pulled Moonlight to a large flat rock. Stepping onto the rock and sensing the horse was ready to bolt, Betsy launched herself into the saddle, dropping one rein, almost sliding off the other side as Moonlight instinctively took off wildly after the other horse. "Heels down, lean back, hang on." Thomas' words ran through her head.

Moonlight raced madly out of control, leaping over rocks and other small obstacles. The thought of falling off at this speed terrified her. "Heels down, lean back, hang on," she repeated, trying to slow the horse by yelling whoa and pulling on a rein. It was as if the horse felt nothing. It ran full tilt, and the rush of wind caused Betsy's eyes to water. Moonlight's mane whipped her face, stinging her eyes until she had to close them. "Heels down, lean back, hang on." Too petrified to cry out, breathlessly she hung onto the pommel and pulled the rein with her left hand.

After a few terrifying moments that seemed like impossibly long minutes, she realized that while the horse was in fact running away with her, she was still securely seated. It took every ounce of her willpower, but finally she forced her right hand to release the pommel and pick up the loose rein. Leaning back and grabbing the reins with both hands, she pulled on them with all her strength, yelling whoa. The horse slowed, tossed its head and slowed some more, but continued on despite her attempts to stop him.

The commotion caused by the wildly racing horse and her yelling attracted the rider's attention, however, and she saw the man stop and turn toward her. His mount, excited by Moonlight's charge, began to prance and surge, but the rider held his horse easily in check.

Moonlight came to a stop only inches from the other horse's nose, and the two animals squared off, attempting to bite at each other, emitting little screams. Betsy quickly noticed that the man appeared not in the least concerned, but spoke in a low voice to his horse, issuing commands which the animal immediately obeyed.

"I, I'm sorry. I, I didn't mean…" Betsy started, breathing hard and not sure if a male would apologize at all.

"Well, I'm glad you decided to wait around," the man said in what she saw as an obvious attempt to put a stranger at ease. "It's lonely for a fellow to ride very far alone."

"Well, if you don't mind, maybe I would like to join you for a spell," Betsy replied gruffly, resettling her hat and remembering to lower her voice to Tom Black's timbre.

The two turned back to the trail and proceeded at a walk, neither speaking for a mile, during which time Betsy wondered if it had been obvious by her wild approach that the horse had been running away with her.

"There's a good campsite someone told me about just up the way a few miles. If we pick up the pace we can make it before dark," the man said. "You up to that?"

"Sure. You first," Tom replied gruffly, spitting for effect while pulling the hat lower and grabbing onto the pommel.

The man studied her for a long minute, which made her even more nervous. "Okay, then. Let's go," he said as he put his horse into an easy lope.

Moonlight seemed content to keep the same pace as the man's horse, which was a great relief to Betsy. She felt infinitely better now that she was in someone's company. Despite the fact that she didn't know this man, his name, or any other thing about him, she felt immensely relieved and safe, for some odd reason, safer than she'd ever felt. In spite of herself and her predicament, relief and happiness swept over her, and she found herself smiling happily before she remembered Thomas' admonition not to smile, no matter what.

The two loped along for a short time and Betsy began to get the feel and rhythm of the horse. She relaxed into the saddle, and despite her best efforts to frown, found herself smiling yet again. She was doing it! She would make it! Her heart soared at her success. Again forgetting Thomas' warning, she looked over at the man beside her, a happy beam lighting up her face. Her grin was short lived, however, when she saw him scrutinizing her. Instantly she cast her eyes askance, and a small frown creased her forehead. She tried to spit once again, but the spittle, blown back by the wind, ran down her chin.

"We'll make camp over yonder," the man said, bringing his horse to a walk. "It'll be dark shortly. We need to get a fire going. I'll gather wood while you hobble the horses."

She had no idea what hobbling was. "Why don't you hobble, and I'll get the firewood?" Betsy said as she thought Tom Black would have.

"Suit yourself," he answered.

Once dismounted she began collecting small sticks and dragging dead branches to the campsite. The lawman unsaddled the horses, hobbling his own.

"You got any hobbles?" he asked as she dragged in a large limb.

"Hobbles?" Tom Black asked in a low-pitched voice, looking at the other horse. "Oh! Those things! No. Forgot 'em, I guess."

"Well, we can use a rope hobble. Hate to do that, but normally it's okay. Where's your rope?"

"Guess I forgot the rope, too," she answered, glad it was dusk and too dark for the man to see her embarrassment.

"You were in a big rush today. Doesn't pay to rush off. People make mistakes when they hurry," the man commented, sounding a bit irritated.

Tom Black remained silent, not responding to the admonishment. Betsy knew the man was right. Everything so far had gone perfectly because she'd planned carefully. But not today.

"What's your name, mister?" her curiosity made her ask.

"Jake Silver."

"You a lawman?" she inquired, unable to mask her nervousness.

"What makes you think so?"

"Just wondered. Thomas said he thought you were."

"That being Thomas DuBonnet?" Jake asked, chuckling.

"Yeah. That's him."

"Got any grub -- Tom Black, is it?"

"That's me," she nodded. "Just some hard, chewy stuff. Man in the store said it was good on the trail."

"Tack. It's okay, I suppose. Since we have a fire tonight I'll share some of my grub with you, if you'd like," Jake offered.

"Thanks, Jake."

Jake heated a can of beans and the two ate in silence. Every time Betsy looked up she could see Jake studying her. Did he know? Could he tell? He couldn't know. She'd smiled only once. Maybe twice. She thought about every incident since she'd joined him. Never had she slipped back into her own voice. She'd tried to walk like Thomas had showed her. She'd even spat several times for effect, which had caused the man to stare and then to stifle a smile. He probably appreciated a good spit. She'd only forgotten herself once that she knew of, and that was when she'd brushed off an area to sit on. Maybe men did that, too, from time to time. She didn't know.

It was a beautiful, but cold night. "The stars! Look! It seems like a body could reach out and touch them!" The statement came out before she realized her gaffe. Maybe he wouldn't notice. Never in her entire life had she seen such brilliant stars.

"Where you from, Tom?" Jake casually asked as he put wood on the fire.

She'd slip back into her role now and play it extra well. He'd forget about the star stuff. "Last I lived in New York City. I was born in Georgia. Moved to New York as a kid."

"You're a kid now, aren't you?"

"I'm seventeen." That much was true.

"All of seventeen, huh?"

"Yep. Born in 1871."

"You come out here to look for your ma?"

"Nope. Made that up. Came out to mine gold, silver, whatever." Why did she just say that? What in tarnation was wrong with her? She supposed being a miner just sounded more masculine than looking for a mother.

Jake Silver sat, looking her over, saying nothing for a spell.

Unable to stand the silence and the scrutiny, fidgety Tom Black spoke, "So, you a lawman or not?"

"Yes, I am. Heading to Prescott to meet with the territorial governor and get duly appointed."

Betsy just nodded her head. "Oh."

"How you gettin' along with that horse, anyway?" Jake asked.

"Better and better. Named him Moonlight," she volunteered, wondering too late if men named their horses.

"Nice name. It's good for an animal to have a name. Shows you care."

"When I was little gi...tyke," she quickly corrected herself, "my mother used to always tell me to catch moonbeams. She said if I caught a moonbeam all my wishes would come true." She paused, then continued, "I think I been searching for moonbeams my whole life. Guess that's why I named the horse as I did." It was the longest Betsy had tried to talk like Tom Black, and her voice began to break. Even though she knew she'd been saying too much, she'd been unable to stop. Her quest for moonbeams had been lifelong. Thinking about it now made her sad. Would a man have volunteered that information? she wondered too late.

"Well, it's best we get to bed. I'll check the horses. You go ahead and roll your blankets out by the fire."

Never having rolled blankets out by a fire, Betsy had no idea as to the best way to proceed, or if there was a special way it should be done. She decided to fiddle around with her saddle and wait for Jake to return so she could see how he rolled his out.

A few moments later he began laying out for the night. Surreptitiously she watched and did the same. Did she detect him smiling?

"Good night, Tom Black."

"Goodnight, Jake." Had she ever said goodnight to a man before? She didn't think so. "I'm glad you invited me to wait for you," she finished, a lump in her throat.

"Anytime, Tom. Anytime."

Exhausted from her physical pounding that morning and the terrifying time alone on the trail, Betsy curled into a tight little ball for warmth, shivered slightly, and fell asleep instantly.

Prescott

JAKE lay awake a long time, periodically stoking the dying embers and adding more firewood. Squatting by the sleeping girl, he laid an extra blanket on her, then gently pushed back the black hat. One look at the extraordinary blonde hair and the angelic face and there remained absolutely no doubt that Tom Black was not Tom Black. He'd had no doubts even before he pushed back the hat, but still he felt compelled to do so for this last bit of evidence. He'd seen the hair before – lying in the hay on the floor of the train car. Seen the girl before, too – in the mercantile in Topeka. Even in the drab, dull dress she'd been wearing the day he first saw her, she'd stood out like no one he'd ever seen before.

Now what the hell was he supposed to do? It was no crime for her to travel as she was. At seventeen, no one would look for her as a runaway. He feared the worst possible outcome for her, however. There were still occasional Indian problems, and plenty of Mexicans who might take advantage of her lived in the Arizona and New Mexico territories. Many outlaws who roamed this area would most definitely take advantage of her.

For now he'd play along. Maybe he could talk some sense into her and convince her to go to Prescott with him. Sighing, he headed to his bedroll. The trip would not be as carefree as he'd hoped, but maybe he could teach her some skills that would keep her alive if she refused to listen to reason and return to the safety of a town.

Still, sleep eluded him. He found himself half angry that he'd have to look out for her, even though he was under no obligation to do so. For some reason he felt compelled to protect the girl, and this scenario made him uneasy. He vacillated between resentment and tenderness for the vulnerable, daring, little blonde. What the hell was wrong with him? A stranger to such sympathetic feelings, he lay sleepless for hours, fretting and fuming over his predicament.

Morning found him absolutely determined to expose her silly lie and reprimand her with a scolding she'd never forget, yet when Tom Black opened her blue eyes and inadvertently smiled at him, his resolve melted. Maybe he'd play along for one more day, just to see what would happen. It would be entertaining if nothing else.

"Better get up and eat a bite. We should've been underway two, three hours ago," he said gruffly.

She didn't answer but hastened to gather her bed roll.

"I already watered and saddled your horse," Jake added. He hadn't wanted to watch what he knew would be a pathetic, desperate attempt on her part at saddling the young, ill-trained, misbehaved horse. He'd have to work with both the horse and rider if the two were going to make it together. At some point she'd undoubtedly leave, though he'd decided the moment he saw her awaken that he'd do his darndest to get her to accompany him to Prescott. He could always arrest her, he supposed.

Again, he fastened her ill-assembled belongings to the back of the saddle, this time explaining how to tie the knots and letting her do so on one side.

"Do I always have to get up and down on the same side of the horse?" she asked, forgetting to use her Tom Black voice.

"No, not particularly. It's good to use both sides. That way if you get in a pinch and have to dismount or mount on a different side than you usually do, the horse won't get scared."

"I'll practice that then," she answered earnestly.

They both now stood on the same side of the animal, with Jake holding the reins. He looked down at the girl and felt his heart skip a beat. Inexplicably his chest tightened and seemed to swell as he took a tiny step toward her to position his hands so she could mount. He could see her cheeks turn red as she nervously glanced at him and then lowered her eyes.

They rode in silence for most of the morning. He noticed that she sat the horse more comfortably and seemed to be at ease when he picked up the pace. "I want to make it to Gallup quickly. If you're up to doing forty or so miles a day we can make it in another two, maybe three days. We didn't get very far yesterday. A night's rest in a hotel room will feel good. Maybe even get a bath," he said when they slowed to a walk after two hours of pace work. The grullo had held his own with Jake's mount, and his admiration for the horse grew.

"I don't think I'll be joining you there."

Jake didn't answer for a long minute. "If you're short on money, Tom, I'd loan you some," he said in an attempt to persuade her. It was the first time that day he'd addressed her by name, finding it ridiculous to continue calling her Tom.

"No. I appreciate the offer, but I, uh, just…" Her voice trailed off momentarily. "I just think I'll stick to the trail."

Reaching out, he firmly grabbed Moonlight's bridle, bringing the horse up short. "Listen, you fool girl," he began, hidden frustration rapidly exploding. "You don't stand a chance by yourself.

Just you be quiet and listen for a minute," he thundered when she started to interrupt. "You want to find your mother, or gold prospect, whichever it is you decide on today, you go right ahead. I'm not going to stop you, but you need to know what you're getting into. Stick around for a few days and I'll teach you what I can about life on the trail. That gold, or your ma, has been waiting for awhile, and it won't hurt either of 'em one bit to wait another day longer." He paused for a moment, releasing the horse. "Now, you can go on and ride outta here like a damned fool and end up being the sorriest woman in the territory, or you can just hold on and let me try to help you. I'm the new U.S. Deputy Marshal here, *TOM*, and I'll find your mother for you. This I promise you." The emphasis on Tom was unmistakable. He knew he'd never let her ride away, but decided it would be better at this point if she chose to stay.

As he watched tears slide down her soft cheeks, it was all he could do to refrain from reaching out to gently brush them away. Little sobs came next, and she moved a delicate hand to hide her face. "I'm so embarrassed," she spoke quietly.

He wanted to tell her that she should be, but he kept the caustic comment to himself.

"I'm sorry. I'm such a fool. I didn't know this would be so difficult," she said, her voice trembling between sobs. "I just need to find my mother. My sister needs her. Everything is just such a, such a…" The words trailed off as her thin shoulders shook.

"Let's get off the trail a bit," Jake suggested, his tone softening. "Looks like there's a good spot a ways over. We can take a break and talk there."

She nodded, and Jake put the horses into a jog, heading toward an area shaded and inviting. Helping her dismount, he tied both animals to a heavy mesquite branch. He would need to call upon his utmost charm and tact, he feared, to get her to accompany him to Prescott. What the hell. He'd arrest her and force her to accompany him if it came down to it. The law was, after all, on his side, wasn't it? It didn't matter. She was going with him whether she wanted to or not.

"So, what's your name? Your *real* name? No more lies." He spoke tersely as he sat and offered her a canteen.

"My name's Elizabeth DuBonnet. I'll tell you the truth, but I'm also telling you that I'm not going back. No matter what you do. If you send me back, I'll just run away again."

"I'm not sending you back, Elizabeth," he said, trying now to speak in a soothing voice, realizing that perhaps he'd come on too strongly. "Calm down now. Just start from the beginning."

She took a deep breath, slowly spilling her sorrowful tale. "I've been living in an orphanage in New York. My mother and sister were there for a bit, but two years ago they got sent west to be married. My mother insisted I was too young to be married, and she lied to the supervisor about my age. They figured I was too old to be adopted, and agreed I was too young to be married, so they kept me there. About a year ago I got a letter from my mama saying she was with a man named John Casey, that the man who was supposed to marry her got killed. She said John Casey was a miner and they were in a town called Wickenburg, out in Arizona. She said she'd send money as soon as she could so I could join her." She paused, wiping her eyes on Jake's proffered neckerchief.

"I was so happy, and then I up and got a letter from my sister, Margaret, who told me she was married to somebody who's a Mormon and she hated it. She wanted Mama and begged for help. I decided I couldn't wait for Mama's money, so I agreed to go west and be married, but all along I planned on running away before I got to where the man was waiting for me."

"Where were you headed?"

"I'm not real sure, but I think it was Colorado. I don't know. I got off the train in Kansas and got on the train you and your horse were on. Thomas Jefferson, well, he's Thomas DuBonnet now, he helped me out. I didn't have enough money, though, to keep buying food all along the way, so I got off when we reached Albuquerque and bought my horse. That's where I first saw you."

"Where'd you come up with the money to finance this expedition, anyway?"

Betsy hesitated. "Well, I borrowed it. Forty-four dollars. But I intend to pay it all back. Every penny. I swear."

"You in the habit of obtaining things you want that way?" Jake smiled inwardly, now knowing he had cause to arrest her for theft if she proved resistant to his plan of taking her to Prescott.

"Never. I would never...borrow like that again."

He nodded, pleased with the information. He liked getting his way, whichever way it took him to do so. "So, you think your mother's in Wickenburg?"

"Yes, I do. I really do. Is that far?"

"Far enough. Tell you what, Elizabeth. Here's a promise I'm making you, and you know that lawmen are bound to keep their word. You know that, don't you? Especially marshals are bound by law," Jake added for emphasis.

She nodded, her tear-streaked face and blue eyes touching him in a way he'd never before been touched.

"I promise you, Elizabeth, that I will find your mother for you. On my word, I will find her if she's in Arizona."

"Would you really?"

"I will. On one condition, though, and that condition is that you let me take you to Prescott. I'm heading that way. I've got to check in with the territorial governor, Governor Zulick. Once I get duly and officially sworn in my search will begin."

"But I have no money to stay anywhere. I'm down to three dollars," Betsy said sadly, tears beginning anew. "I spent so much money on my horse and saddle and then I had to get food at those train stops. I didn't think the trip would take so long or that food would cost so much."

"I got plenty of money," Jake volunteered. "How's this offer. I'll make you a loan, and you can pay me back when you get yourself a job or strike it rich in the mines…whichever comes first. How's that?"

"That could be a long time. I don't know…" Her voice trailed off, and Jake could see indecisiveness gathering. He thought her honesty and trepidation quaint and reassuring.

"Elizabeth, you've got to trust me. I won't let you down. In fact, I'll teach you things you need to know to survive on the trail. If you get to Prescott and decide you can't wait for me to find your mother, at least you'll be prepared to take care of yourself."

"That's fair," she said, smiling weakly. "You can call me Betsy, by the way."

"Okay, Betsy. Let's mount up and make town. You'll feel better after a good night's sleep and a hot bath. I'll treat you to dinner, too, how's that?"

"Jake, I'll never be able to repay you if you keep spending money on me like this."

"Well, that means you'll just be indebted and have to wash my shirts now and then." He smiled and gave her a wink. He enjoyed her blush and laughter, even though he wondered why he'd made such a fool statement.

The next weeks proved more difficult than Jake expected as they journeyed toward Prescott. He found Betsy to be an eager, quick learner, however. Her horsemanship skills developed rapidly, and in short order she rode with confidence, even showing off from time to time. Sometimes she became uncommonly quiet and preoccupied, the tiny frown on her brow indicating worry, but when she smiled, showing those perfect white teeth, he could feel his heart thud and his chest tighten. Sometimes she stood so very close to him, much closer than needed, and these were times he felt his throat constrict and his chest swell. Damn, what was wrong with him? Alarmed that his arms began to warm to the idea of wrapping around the girl, he forced them to drop to his gun belt while he gazed at the horizon and scowled, trying to ignore her shoulder as it brushed his arm. He didn't know what was happening. He just wanted to hold her and, well, kiss her. Nothing wrong in that, he counseled himself, except for the fact that he was a lawman and her caretaker, not a beau. That would amount to a conflict of interest if there ever was one. He'd known his share of women who were more than willing. Why was he so smitten with the most innocent, naive creature he'd ever met?

In better weather he indulged her desire to camp along the route, so concerned was she about spending his money, but every few days he insisted on staying in a hotel or inn. He'd spent more than his share of nights looking at the stars and knew he was bound to spend many more nights doing so as he traveled the breadth and width of northern Arizona. He always paid for two rooms and was more than happy to let her eat in her room. He thought she looked ridiculous masquerading as a male, especially now that he knew her true identity. And always, daily, he kept reminding himself that he must not become attached to the girl. She would undoubtedly choose to go with her mother when he found the woman. Besides, he had plenty of other business to tend to.

He had a slew of arguments prepared for himself when he found his gaze wandering to the winsome girl who rode beside him. Even her shaggy hair seemed wonderful. From what he could tell, she appeared to be unaware of his growing interest in her, although on occasion he found her furtively watching him. He could think of no reason why she would do so. Probably scared he'd send her to jail.

Often, sitting by the campfire in the evening, talk would turn to their childhoods, and hers seemed far more colorful having lived on a plantation in the South than his boyhood spent on a cattle ranch in Fort Worth. The mystery which she seemed unable to explain involved how her French mother had come to be on a plantation in the deep South. "We never talked about that," she answered. "I don't know. I just know that Mama had lots of gentlemen callers, but then one day she packed our bags and said we were leaving. I think one of the men maybe hurt Margaret. I don't know. I think I was too young to notice anything."

"You're depending a lot, Betsy, on me finding your mother. What if she's left Arizona? Miners are notorious for packing up and leaving the moment they hear of another lode being struck."

"I'll find Margaret then."

"Where's she? You got any idea?"

"Someplace where Mormons live is all I know."

"Betsy," Jake paused. He didn't want to ruin her hopes with reality. "Betsy, I'm not saying you won't find your mother or Margaret, I'm just suggesting you need a plan, just in case."

"Well, about all that's left is to find a moonbeam. I'd get my wishes then," she answered, smiling sadly.

He watched her as she stared into the fire.

"Well, I hear Prescott's a nice town," he added, trying to ease her worries. "You can find a job there and have a good life. And if your mama's in Arizona, I'll find her, so don't you concern yourself about that."

"I hope you're right, Jake."

The trip across Arizona proved more difficult that spring than he thought it would. The terrain was passing fair with primarily low, rolling hills and no steep summits to surmount, but the altitude often kept the early spring weather decidedly cold and windy.

The land, green with sage and scattered juniper, was mostly wide-open country with only occasional rock ridges which were seldom much help for protection given the wind direction. The first real rainy, windy day left Betsy visibly shivering, her face pinched in discomfort and her fingers numb. He wrapped his heavy coat around her, making her keep her frozen hands inside the coat's long woolen sleeves while he led Moonlight. He wore his suit jacket and was chilled but not uncomfortable.

A couple of shots of good mash whiskey that night upon reaching Holbrook warmed him thoroughly. He knew that camping out in the extreme cold would be too much for Betsy despite her protestations otherwise, so he made certain to make sufficient mileage to reach towns, inns, or stations along the route as often as possible. He picked up a boy's duster for her in Winslow even though she was adamantly opposed to the purchase, but continuing cold weather saw the coat get plenty of use.

Yet other days grew quite warm, sometimes downright hot, and they both shed outer layers. The horses also relaxed and got off the muscle brought on by cold and wind. The two talked more on these warm sunny days, and Betsy asked questions nonstop: questions about the West mostly, but also questions about Jake and his family, two things he didn't care to discuss.

He held views on certain controversial subjects that weren't popular, and once after a big family feud where his father refused to speak to him for many weeks, he'd resolved to keep his opinions to himself about such matters. It wasn't long afterward that he took up driving broomtail.

He could see that Betsy thirsted for information about what she considered "normal" families, so he relinquished his taciturnity, but talked mostly about his sister Sophy.

"Is she younger or older than you?"

"Older. But she's the one closest in age to me. She's seven years older."

"Is she married?"

"Nah. Sophy teaches school in Fort Worth. She was sweet on some guy when I was last home, though. Thought he might ask her to marry him. Haven't heard nothing, so I'm not sure how that all turned out."

"Don't you miss your family?"

"Miss them? Not really. I think on them some, but I'm not lonely for them, if that's what you mean. I grew up pretty much by myself as a kid 'cause my brothers were quite a bit older."

"I miss my mom so much," Betsy said, sadness creeping into her voice. "And Margaret. I never had a friend except for Margaret. I'll be so glad to find them."

Sensing her despondency, he quickly picked up their pace until the next town came into sight.

Approaching Flagstaff and freezing weather at the seven-thousand-foot level, Jake wondered if he'd been in his right mind to accept the position as marshal for northern Arizona, but as they approached Flagstaff, beautiful ponderosa pine and the snow-capped view of the San Francisco Peaks replaced the windswept landscape. With the change, the journey became more mountainous and the spring-night temperatures regularly dipped below freezing.

He now knew, without a doubt, that Betsy would never have survived the trip alone but would have succumbed early on to hypothermia. One night out of Flagstaff when they were forced to sleep outside, he built a shelter from pine boughs to break the wind, but even then the girl shook with cold in her sleep. He'd been compelled to lie beside her and wrap the waiflike girl in his arms in an effort to warm her, not leaving her side until daybreak. To his knowledge she never awakened, for she never spoke of it.

Despite the difficulty of the journey brought on by the high altitude and cool weather, for him the distance to Prescott diminished all too quickly, and in late April the two rode into the town where Jake assumed their paths would part.

DuBonnet

EVEN before the train arrived in Topeka, Thomas DuBonnet knew what he must do. It wasn't a matter of *having* to do it, really. It was that he knew what he *wanted* and *needed* to do. If little Tom Black had the courage to ride into the sunset and face an uncertain future, why was he hiding in the past? Betsy had shared her dreams with him, and in so doing had reawakened possibilities he knew awaited him if only he had the courage to pursue them. He swelled with pride when he thought of the intrepid decisions he'd made to help her, to touch her hair, to even speak to her. Hanging offenses all, yet he'd been brave enough to do them. Maybe he wasn't such a coward after all.

Thomas kept a well-hidden secret. He would take his secret and the train from Topeka to Arizona where he would dedicate himself to finding the wandering girl; then he would rebuild his own life. He was prepared to risk all to fulfill this rescue mission and his dream of being a man of good standing, a real man who was not afraid of every gun-toting Reb sympathizer who sneered at him when he walked down the street.

Prescott seemed a good place to start, at least as good as any, and he'd talk to the new marshal while there. The man seemed tolerant, even kind, despite his imposing demeanor, but Thomas knew the marshal would not take kindly to what had occurred in the train car. Still, it was the right thing to do.

He'd been to Prescott more than a dozen times on the train run. It was the first town he'd walked in where people had not openly shunned him, where he'd not been expected to step off the boardwalk into the street when white folk passed by, although he had anyway. He'd not had to shuffle his feet, remove his hat, nod his head and grovel, saying, "Yes suh, no suh." Men of his color were shot in many towns for simply being in sight, or for letting their eyes linger too long on a white face.

Thomas knew it might be possible that he'd face death when he revealed his secret to the marshal, although he doubted that, but after watching Betsy wave goodbye as the train pulled out of Albuquerque, he firmly believed it was worth the risk.

For some days he kept to himself in Topeka, planning carefully. He must not be caught. If he were, he'd certainly be hanged or shot, no questions asked.

A two-day horseback ride from Topeka, hidden deep in the cleft of a rock, lay a bag filled with silver and gold coins. They were his now; he'd found them, and years had passed since then.

After leaving the South, unable to make a living as a sharecropper in the aftermath of the war where he'd served in the Union Army, he journeyed north in hopes of finding a better life. Quickly disappointed at the plight of the black man there also, he headed west. It was on this trip that he came across the bag, apparently dropped by bandits in the course of a stagecoach holdup, or maybe even a train robbery.

A strong believer that safety lie in solitude, he'd stayed away from the main routes when he traveled to avoid potential trouble, and had forged his own ambling path. As he rambled through the countryside, near one of his campsites he'd come upon the "pot of gold." It lay in the brush in such a way that he had no doubt it'd fallen, or had been dropped, by a fleeing horseman. He sat for some time, running his fingers through the eagles and double eagles, sifting, squeezing, lovingly caressing each coin, almost choking with excitement. He'd never seen so much money, and at first he thought his every prayer had been answered. But upon reflection, he knew better than to carry this much money. Plenty smart enough to know that a black man with a bag of cash would be marked for death; he figured assassins wouldn't even ask questions. So he buried the loot, hiding the money so well that he had little doubt it would still be there, taking only a handful to help get him to the nearby town of Topeka. He never returned to the site.

So, he would retrieve his cache and go west, the only place where a man of color might find peace, and even that was not guaranteed.

He spent several days fashioning a sash in the style of a cummerbund that would wrap securely about his midsection. He made it big enough to spread the money evenly. He'd carry some in his pockets and more hidden in his saddlebag, as any man might. He'd buy some clothes, no new ones lest they attract undue attention, and he'd buy a horse, not a mule. A horse was more respectable, yet on second thought, he realized a horse might attract attention. If he rode a mule, no one would notice. A black man on a mule would be more acceptable. Disappointed, he consoled himself with the knowledge that mules were stronger and more surefooted than horses. Someday he'd have a horse, though.

As he sewed his money sash, his thoughts turned to what he would do in Prescott. His money would not last forever, although it could if he lived as he lived now, on a subsistence level working a low-paying job. But what, then, was the point? What would have changed for him?

Mining seemed alluring, but he knew it to be spotty and unreliable. Maybe he could get a job again as a porter on the train. Better, he was good with animals, so perhaps he could hire on as a ranch hand. He'd heard there were many cowboys of color, both black and Mexican, in the west. Some even served as deputies. But first he would find the girl. He felt guilty beyond measure for letting her go off by herself. Perhaps he should never have gotten involved in helping her in the first place, but he was responsible now, whether he liked it or not. Humming as he sewed, he dared to picture his coming days of prosperity and happiness.

Early one morning, three weeks after returning to Topeka, Thomas DuBonnet left town, unnoticed, on a two-day trek to retrieve the stolen cash. He'd return to Topeka only to catch the AT & SF, hastening to get out of Kansas as quickly as possible, an area that seemed to grow more lawless by the day.

Being a black man and traveling alone required that he avoid people as much as possible, and certainly he must avoid men on horseback at all costs. Too many desperadoes used black men for target practice. He planned to ride straight through, stopping only briefly for rest at places he knew would provide safe haven.

The journey brought back memories, some not so pleasant. It seemed that all his memories involved him running, hiding, never standing proud like a man. He'd never stood his ground except once, and that had been during the war. He'd enlisted in the Union Army, and even though well underage, he hadn't been turned away. Because of his youth he'd been assigned as a messenger between camps and to help care for horses. To protect him if he were caught by the Rebs, he hadn't been issued a uniform, but rather given clean clothes and his first pair of new brogans and socks. The war had been good for him, despite the horrendous mayhem and bloodshed he'd witnessed on a regular basis. Along the way he'd met other men of color who were proud, brave men, not ashamed of being black, not fearful of every white man who looked their way. They fought for their dignity and freedom, but if he were honest, Thomas had only enlisted to escape the drudgery of the fields.

His turning point had been Gettysburg, when he'd heard the great President Lincoln deliver his address. But the inspiration lasted only a short while. After the war things grew even worse, impossible, for black people in the South. Angry Southerners looked for any excuse to lynch a black man, and when the whole white population of the South was suffering from the effects of the great war, being a black man demanding rights did not bode well.

He'd cleared out, leaving behind a wife and child. He felt great shame in this. So much shame that he'd returned once, on his journey west, to make amends and try to talk his wife into joining him, but she was with another man by that time. She'd looked at him as he stood on the broken-down porch and said nothing. He heard his son begin to cry as she closed the door.

Thomas wiped an involuntary tear from his eye as he remembered his wife's large, brown eyes peering at him. No hate. No love. Nothing came from them except indifference.

Wanting to forget the past, he tried to enjoy the vista before him, but he found it impossible to relax and do so when he constantly had to search his back trail for other riders. He'd only feel relief when he finally settled onboard the train headed west. Smiling, he pictured himself buying his ticket and taking a seat. He'd have money to be able to eat at the stops.

He thought of little Betsy and her perilous journey, shaking his head in disbelief that he'd taken such a chance by helping a white girl. It wasn't his nature to take chances. But since meeting her, his life seemed to be filling up with risk taking and chances. He smiled again, thinking of the changes he planned to make for himself – all because of her.

First thing, he'd find the marshal and square things. Fess up to helping her and tell him what he knew. He'd probably get a tongue lashing from the man, but he didn't think he'd be arrested or hanged. He'd heard Prescott didn't do so much hanging, anyway. Still, you never knew. After confessing, he'd begin his search and not stop until he found her, dead or alive. He hoped the marshal would help, if at all possible. Thomas often prayed that she was alive and well. Should harm come to her, he knew he'd hold himself responsible.

The two days passed in a sorrowful blur, his thoughts taking him far from the road he traveled. Suddenly, in the late afternoon of the second day, he realized he'd arrived. Dismounting, he tied the mule and sat for a spell, making sure that no one would come unexpectedly upon him. He recognized the rocky outcropping where he'd hidden the money, although weeds had done their best to disguise the area. As evening approached, he ventured closer. Was the pouch there? At first he didn't see the crevice, as dirt and weeds had moved into the space. But on an almost frantic, closer inspection, he saw the end of the rainbow and his pot of gold. Quickly, he dug the bag out, bloodying his fingers and scraping his knuckles. Yes, it was there. All of it, he guessed more than five thousand dollars.

He sauntered back to the campsite, trying to appear casual and unconcerned, but keeping a wary eye about him. Waiting until dark, he spread the money, then carefully stowed it in his sash and saddlebags. After securing the sash around his waist, he decided to sleep until first light, then he would retrace his route to Topeka one last time. He could begin a new life, for he'd surely found one of Miss Betsy's moonbeams.

"I'm coming for you, Miss Betsy. Thomas DuBonnet will help you," he said quietly as he stretched out on the cold ground. He started no fire. He didn't want to attract any fellow travelers or curiosity seekers. His mule stood close by. He must find water for the animal tomorrow, which meant he'd either have to venture close to a settlement, or find a stream.

He awoke in the early, gray dawn, immediately reveling in happiness that no one had sneaked into his camp and slit his throat during the night. Dusting off his clothes, he untied the mule and began the journey he knew in his heart would truly set him free.

The Marshal Arrives

JAKE Silver's arrival in Prescott as the new U.S. Deputy Marshal gave the town the occasion for much gossip, controversy, and a series of social activities. He'd hoped to have Betsy established in a boarding house before Governor Zulick got wind of his arrival, but luck was not on his side.

Riding into town, Jake knew the two made a striking pair, and he figured that was because no one could be certain at first glance if Betsy was a male or female, or whether she was his companion, wife, relative, or a fugitive. They'd barely entered the town when word spread like a telegraphed message that something strange was going on. People discreetly, and indiscreetly, peeped out their windows or directed their steps to see where the pair might alight.

Jake knew that temporary living arrangements had been made for him, but Betsy had no place to stay. He felt it best to get her situated immediately so that she could avoid unfair scrutiny. It quickly became clear from the strangers he questioned, that the town offered several boarding houses from which to choose, but only one that everyone endorsed, so they headed that direction.

He could see his companion becoming flustered by all the staring and pointing as they rode along the street. Women seemed particularly fascinated with the two, and he could only imagine the unfair speculation being circulated. He hadn't thought about these things or he would've made arrangements in advance, wiring from a town along the route. He could only hope for a vacancy at one of the dwellings.

They were in luck, and Miss Virginia Hall, according to the townspeople, a prosperous and well-liked businesswoman, took one look at Betsy and greeted her with open arms. The three stood in the quiet, lavender-scented parlor filled with silky-looking, fragile furnishings. Jake stood silently by while the older woman fussed over Betsy as though she were long-lost kin. He could see Betsy's reserve melt and a smile visit her dirty, tanned face.

"You must be exhausted, dear, after such a trip! Just look at how brown you are! Heavens! How long have you been traveling?"

"About two months," Betsy answered proudly.

"I must hear all about your adventure, but first I'm sure you'd like to see your room and have a lovely bath. I see you travel light. I have some clothes I think will fit, if you'd like. Of course, dear, I don't wish to presume, so please tell me if I'm being too bold."

"Thank you for your kindness, Miss Hall."

The woman finally turned her attention to Jake, who'd been standing idly by, twirling his hat, wondering how long someone could carry on with a complete stranger. "As for you, sir, you may settle up with me at another time. I've already heard that you're the new marshal, so I'm giving you the benefit of the doubt. I'm confident that you'll be around to take care of Ms. DuBonnet's accommodations?"

"Yes, ma'am."

"Very well. I know you're expected elsewhere. Will you be taking Ms. DuBonnet's horse? Perhaps she'll be keeping it here or boarding it at the stables?"

He caught Betsy's worried frown. She owned the animal, so he had no inclination or right to take it from her. He gave her a nod and allowed her to speak for herself.

"I'd like to keep the horse here, if that's okay, Jake," she said, turning to Miss Hall. "I can take care of it. I can help pay for his keep, maybe, by working in the barn."

"That is utterly unthinkable, dear. We'll work something out for you, I'm sure. What say you, Marshal Silver?"

"It's Betsy's horse, Miss Hall. Bought and paid for by her alone." He saw Miss Hall look approvingly toward the girl. "She should keep the animal, and I'll cover its expense until she gets on her feet and can provide for it herself."

"Well decided, Marshal Silver. I highly admire a man who allows a woman her independence. Now, you need to be off, I'm certain. But first, might I inquire how long Miss DuBonnet will be staying?"

Both stood speechless. Neither had thought about this.

"We can always go month to month, of course. It's a wee bit more expensive, but…"

"Yes. That's a fine idea. Month to month. That way, Betsy," Jake said turning to her, "when I find your mother you'll be free to leave."

"Oh, is your poor mother missing, dear? I'm so terribly sorry," interjected Miss Hall.

Betsy smiled weakly in response. Jake noted she didn't seem happy, and he wondered what the devil was the matter with her. She'd traveled over two thousand miles to find her mother and now she appeared to be, well, indifferent.

"I'll be getting a job as soon as I can, Jake. I don't want to be a burden. You've helped me so much, and I'm thankful. I'll pay you back as soon as I can. You know that."

"Told you before, Betsy, you're no burden. Don't worry about the money."

"Will I..." Betsy hesitated. "Will I be seeing you...around town or...?"

"Absolutely. I'll come by in a day or two after you've had a chance to get settled."

He could see she was reluctant to see him go.

"Okay," she answered, turning quickly away, a catch in her voice. He feared tears would come again, so he nodded to Miss Hall and left.

Well, he'd made it. He'd delivered her safely to Prescott. He could wash his hands of her. Now there was no need for him to continue to protect her. He'd pay for six months' rent for her and Moonlight's keep, and it'd be worth every penny not to have to be responsible for her. In six months she'd be on her feet and able to care for herself. He'd done his good deed for the year. For several years.

No matter how he tried to muster relief that a great burden had been lifted from him, he didn't feel that way at all. He felt distinctly lonely without her there beside him, smiling and looking so beautiful as she managed to do every single day, dirty face and all. And he worried for her. She was so, so endearing, and all alone. But, he adamantly reminded himself, she was *not* his problem or responsibility any longer. Task accomplished. Nevertheless, he led her horse to the back of the property, unsaddled him, thoroughly rubbed him down, and then gave him plenty of feed. "You're quite an animal, Moonlight. Lucky for you I'm quite a trainer or you'd be horsemeat if anyone else had bought you."

Finally, he headed to the governor's headquarters. He'd be staying there for the next two weeks while being introduced, shown off, and subtly interrogated. After that, he'd have to find a temporary place to live before seeking something permanent. Probably best not to go to Miss Hall's establishment. He preferred hotels, anyway. More private with fewer questions.

"You look perfect for the part, Marshal Silver. Had you shown up in a suit I would have fired you immediately. We need a man who demands respect, and you look like a serious piece of work." So spoke Governor Zulick as he eyed Silver's dusty clothes and two-day growth of stubble.

"I'm afraid you caught me before I could make myself presentable, Governor," Jake answered politely, uncomfortable at receiving praise or undue amounts of attention.

"Nonsense. You look like a man should."

The two exchanged a few pleasantries before a servant showed Jake his room and described the layout of the town. "There's a barber, and we have a bath house, or we can draw a hot bath for you here, sir."

Jake wondered if that was a not-so-subtle suggestion about the condition of his trail-worn person. "Thanks. That sounds good. Let me put my horse up and I'll be obliged to have a bath drawn right here."

"There's someone to attend to your horse, Marshal."

"No one attends to my horse but me. Thank you, anyway."

"As you wish, Mr. Silver."

The next few days rolled on with an endless line of community businessmen and officers from the fort stopping by to meet the new U.S. Deputy Marshal. Perfectly aware it had been four days since he'd seen Betsy, and that he'd told her it would only be a day or two, he thought perhaps it would be easier to make the break if he just stayed away altogether. While he never stopped thinking of her, he kept occupied with endless social obligations and introductions. Maybe he'd see her one last time. He'd ask her to accompany him to the governor's reception for him - - yet another excuse to hold a gathering to honor his being duly and officially appointed Arizona's U.S. Deputy Marshal.

As he approached the whitewashed gate in front of Miss Hall's boarding house, he halted, stunned. The most dazzling, beautiful girl he'd ever seen came stepping out onto the porch.

Betsy stood completely transformed from the dusty, grubby, winsome trail hand, and had become a beauty beyond compare. Miss Hall had evidently evened out the girl's shaggy hair, he noted, and it now hung, nearly chin length, a blue bow decorating her white-blonde tresses. She wore a dress whose color, he could tell even from a distance, matched her arresting blue eyes. The dress had some kind of white lacey-looking cuffs and collar, fit snugly at her tiny waist, then fell loosely about her slender frame. Sudden warmth rushed through him just looking at her. She looked delectable, and he stared, slack jawed and plain stunned. He'd thought her irresistible before, but now she appeared downright heavenly. Scrumptious. Better than anything he'd ever laid his eyes on.

"Betsy. You look…you look right nice," he stammered, entering through the gate, unable to say the words he wanted for fear of sounding like a dandy.

"Thank you, Jake." She smiled brightly, a slight blush coloring her cheeks.

They both stood looking at one another, speechless a moment, neither sure what to say.

Betsy finally broke the impasse. "How are things going? You must be very busy."

"Yes. Busy being busy. That's it so far. It's been just one person after another poking their fool heads in to get a gander at me."

"I trusted you hadn't forgotten me." She blushed even more.

"You know better, I hope." He felt a bit ashamed. That had been exactly what he'd been trying to do for days.

She smiled again and appeared somewhat flustered, which drove him near to distraction.

"I was wonderin' if you'd want to go to a reception with me tonight? It'll be just a bunch of men and women gabbing and eating sweetmeats, drinking tea out of tiny cups, sipping wine out of glasses that break if you don't set them down real gentle, and stuff like that."

"Do you suppose I'll look okay dressed as I am?" Betsy asked.

"Nonsense, girl," Miss Hall broke in from behind the screen door. "I have just the thing for you."

Betsy smiled apologetically at Jake and sighed. "Thank you, Miss Hall," she said, turning to the door, but seeing only an empty passageway.

"I'll come by about five o'clock and fetch you. I'd like to show you around town a bit too, if you've a mind to."

"That would be grand, Jake. I'd be honored."

He winked at her, then made his way down the steps and through the gate to his horse. "All right, then, until five." This was a new Betsy, a prim and proper one, he mused as he mounted his horse and tipped his hat in salute. He sort of missed the ragamuffin gal he'd known on the trail, but it was good to know she'd fit into Prescott society with nary a trouble. He figured the Betsy he knew was still in there somewhere. He hoped she was. But he sure enjoyed looking at the goddess she now appeared to be.

When he returned at five, he once again stood mesmerized as she entered the parlor. Dressed in all white, he guessed she wore a simple, yet elegant gown of satin, decorated with tiny pearl buttons and a small red rose mysteriously fastened to the bodice near her throat.

Marshal Jake Silver wasn't the star of the reception that night, but rather Elizabeth DuBonnet who quickly won the admiration and approval of the guests. She'd also won the prerequisite jealousy and dislike of the young women competing for the eligible Marshal Silver's favor. Jake, astounded by Betsy's poise and quiet self-assurance as she met the governor's other guests, wondered where she'd developed such self-confidence and aplomb. The evening proved to be a social success for her, and Jake was mostly glad about that, for now opportunities would arise for her that might not have otherwise. Now he could travel on assignments and not worry about her being alone and ignored. Quickly he corrected this thinking, reminding himself it was not his concern if she sat alone, ignored, or if opportunities came her way. At least she was safe, thanks to him. He could see, too, that she might not remain single very long, what with the number of officers greeting her in their pompous, hand-kissing manner. Though he felt a bit ruffled, he didn't intervene.

"Marshal Silver? I'm Genevieve Armstrong. It's such a pleasure to make your acquaintance. I've heard so much about you," the young woman before him gushed, placing her hand upon his hard bicep. "Oh my, oh my. You must be terribly strong."

Flushed, Jake nodded and backed slowly away from the attractive, bosomy brunette. "Nice to meet you, ma'am." Noting that Betsy had captured a young officer's full attention, he found his way to the porch and joined the other escapees enjoying their cigars and discussing the goings on in Washington and the eastern seaboard.

As he returned Betsy to the boarding house that evening, she sat close to him in the carriage, smiling happily and talking animatedly.

"Betsy," he injected during a lull in her chatter. "I gotta talk to you about something." He paused for effect. "I'll be leaving town shortly for a tour of the territory. I gotta get your word that you'll stay put and not take off while I'm gone. I promised you I'd look for your mother, and I'm going to just as soon as I return. I'd begin looking now, but the governor has asked me to go to Freeman for…" he paused, not sure what to say. "I won't be gone long. Can you promise me you'll stay?"

Did she hesitate? "Of course, I'll stay. I'll look for a job while you're away. Miss Hall says there's lots of respectable positions here for a girl."

They continued up the street in silence. He noticed her mood had dampened.

"Thank you, Jake. I had a wonderful time," she said as he walked her to the door where Miss Hall was waiting, beaming with pride at her darling guest. "It's the best time I've ever had, except for maybe when we were traveling - -" she stopped, appearing uncertain.

"Good night, Betsy. I'll see you again. Soon I hope."

She smiled when he winked at her as Miss Hall closed the door. He walked to the carriage knowing with an absolute certainty that he had to get out of town. He couldn't take seeing her anymore. Being close to her and not holding her was becoming unbearable. Seeing her tonight with other men bowing and acting like regular jackasses, kissing her hand and showering her with compliments, had nearly driven him mad. She was a child, he kept telling himself. Seventeen, so she said, although he recognized that she'd conducted herself like a mature woman this evening. He had to leave. He'd go tomorrow. He'd head to Freeman. Back to Topeka. Anywhere. He didn't care. He needed to clear his head once and for all time of her. He needed to get back to his old self. He liked the way he'd been - carefree, unfettered, and ready to roll the dice on life. He liked not worrying about shaving so's he could look good. He liked not caring if anyone cared. Damn.

He'd send her a message before he left and remind her of her promise to stay put. When he returned he vowed he'd find her mother and then send the girl on her way. This would be easy, and he had no doubt his plan would be for the best.

Yep. The last thing he needed was her hanging on him like a millstone.

Into Navajo Country

TWO days after the governor's shindig, Jake Silver left Prescott headed for Navajo country and Freeman, a small community of white settlers along the Arizona and Utah borders where Indian raids reportedly had been a problem. After reading the skimpy reports that had filtered in to the governor's office, he had trouble believing Indians were the culprits. But who else would bother to trouble the settlement? The only other community within a day's ride of Freeman appeared to be a small Mormon community situated in the canyon. He'd go there and try to find out who was stirring the pot.

Determined to make the break clean, he decided not to send a note to Betsy. He simply left. He needed to become the marshal he'd been hired on to be. As far as he was concerned, he'd made the break with Betsy final.

A day or so out of Prescott, the big pines began to thin. The country remained green, but drier, sandier tracks, dotted with scrubby juniper filled the landscape. Sparse, windswept areas became more frequent. At this pace, he'd make Tuba City in four days, maybe less. He'd rest his horse for a day if needed and then head due north. It would be a hazardous, full day's ride, but he wanted to stop at a new outpost struggling to get a foothold that he'd heard about in Prescott. Good to know about these places for future reference.

Being part Arab, his horse seemed to have no limits as far as burning up the miles went. Once the animal found its pace it continued tirelessly, seldom breaking a sweat. Several times Jake stopped anyway to check the horse's respiration and body heat, but always the animal proved stable and eager to return to the trail. He hesitated to let the horse run so freely. It needed to be ready for a prolonged burst of speed should that become necessary, yet he also wanted to accumulate distance as quickly as possible. What, he wondered, would mark the mile where he would forget entirely about Betsy? Where would he be when thoughts of her faded like a colored kerchief worn and washed too often? He counted on it not taking too long.

Mile after mile the horse ran effortlessly. It felt good to be in the saddle with only the wind and sun for companionship. This was life as it should be, he reasoned, and at times he could hardly contain the happiness he felt. Life just didn't get much better.

By his reckoning, he easily covered almost seventy miles the day he reached Tuba City. He marveled at the change in vegetation, for after leaving the greenery of the high country, the landscape became mostly level grassland for a long stretch. Cliffs rose from the earth in the distance, possibly signifying a canyon. The farther east he traveled, less grass and rockier ground became the norm. Occasional rock outcroppings appeared out of nowhere, it seemed. The trail took him into a shallow canyon which he followed for a mile or better before emerging into a grassless, hilly area bordered by flat-top mesas along one side. Small peaks, like miniature mountains, erupted from the dirt landscape. The soil, now red instead of sandy colored, made the earth look hard and desolate. Tuba City looked hard and desolate also - dusty and uninviting.

The horse snorted in protest when he finally brought it to a walk, but Jake was tired after being in the saddle for close to a week, the last two days covering ground at an unbelievable pace. He'd rub the horse down and secure it well. After surveying his surroundings, he decided he'd sleep in the stall. He didn't like the mixture of animosity and envy cast his way as residents of the largely Indian community surreptitiously studied his mount. Jake fully understood their animosity toward white men. He bore no hard feelings about it, but by his stern glare, he let the onlookers know they'd have more trouble on their hands than they'd bargained for if anyone even touched the animal.

"You passing through or staying awhile?" a tall, well-dressed white man asked.

"That depends," Jake answered.

"Let me introduce myself. I'm John Stillwell. I'm a member of the Mormon community settled here."

Jake nodded in recognition.

"Seeing that badge you're wearing, I'm assuming you're the new U.S. Deputy Marshal," the man said.

"Indeed I am. Jake Silver."

"We'd be honored, Marshal Silver, if you'd spend the night in our community. I think you'll find our accommodations superior to anything here. We're several miles out of town."

"Thank you, Mr. Stillwell. I believe I'll take you up on that offer."

"My wagon's over yonder. I'll fetch it and you can follow me on out. It's a ways, but a pleasant journey, nonetheless."

Jake remounted and waited for his host to come by. He fell in behind the wagon and followed as the man drove the team to the Mormon settlement well east of town. He couldn't help but wonder why white folks had settled here. This was Indian country, land the Indians had always lived on and owned, except for the brief time when they'd been incarcerated at Fort Sumner. White people had taken just about everything from these people, and now they wouldn't leave them alone on their own land.

Word spread quickly in the small community that a visitor had arrived, and folks made much ado because of it. Jake's arrival served as the occasion for a number of people to gather that evening after supper at Stillwell's large, partially built home. After preliminary introductions, it took no time for members of the group to voice their concerns about their Navajo neighbors.

"I'm tellin' ya, they got no respect for a man's property," one harried settler, George Burdick, complained as his wife nodded vigorously while he spoke. "They come right through the fencing and help themselves to my livestock, my wife's chickens. Even my garden is under siege. I'm surprised, and thankful, they ain't grabbed my girl yet."

"They're grabbing young girls up in Freeman, according to what we've heard," a righteous-looking man dressed in finery explained for Jake's benefit.

"Three young girls been snatched up by these heathens. Somebody's gotta stop 'em," another elder added.

"Now, we don't know that the Indians took the girls," Stillwell counseled. "Anybody could've taken them. Perhaps no one took them and they simply ran off."

"That's what happens when a man don't keep his womenfolk secured," another man huffed.

The talk continued for some time. Jake noticed no one asked his advice or help, rather they just seemed to need an opportunity to air grievances and worries.

"Might the soldiers from the fort come and stop this nonsense?" someone asked.

"Hear hear! Splendid idea," a second man shouted.

All focused now on the marshal in their midst.

"I think this is probably out of their jurisdiction," Jake cautiously volunteered. "This is considered by most," he hesitated a moment, wanting to use the right tone and approach, "to be rightfully Indian territory. There's talk that this will be an official reservation, if the proposal hasn't already been signed." He hesitated to tell them they'd probably have to pick up and leave, that they should in fact move on and had no business settling where they did. Despite his own family's homestead, Jake firmly held the unpopular opinion that the white man had often violently, and illegally, taken Indian land, forcing the diminishing race to live on the most squalid plots available, land in which white people saw no value. Even then, Indians were often moved again if it was discovered that the area was rich in ore of any kind. His sympathies were not with this community, although he could see that the people felt decidedly differently and saw no wrong in claiming land for which no legal paper deed had been obtained.

"Well, what about the kidnapping of young white girls?"

"That's another matter, and one I guarantee you I'll look into when I get to Freeman," Jake assured them. "Try to keep an open mind about this, if you can. It may not be Indians causing the trouble at all. It could be...." He slowed and hoped the sentence would die a natural death. He was not so lucky.

"Yes? Who else could it be? Mexicans? Outlaws?"

"I suppose that's possible," Jake said, not wanting to go further.

"Well, who else?" Stillwell asked as the others peered at Jake, waiting for an answer.

"Now, I'm not saying for certain, but there are rumors about those Mormons who take on more than one wife, and it's possible...." Jake could see by the horrified expressions surrounding him that his idea was less than poorly received.

Fortunately, Stillwell interrupted the proceedings. "Well, I think we should disperse for the evening. I'm sure Marshal Silver is very tired from his long journey. He's given us his word that he'll look into the problems in Freeman, and that's all we can reasonably expect at this time until we know more."

Slowly the assembly filed out in twos and threes; a few small groups stood on the dimly lit porch in heated conversation for some time, leaving Stillwell and Jake alone in the unfinished meeting hall.

"Sorry I brought that up," Jake said.

"Not at all, Marshal. What you say is, unfortunately, highly possible. I do think the polygamy practiced by many of our members is a black mark upon our Mormon faith. It troubles me deeply, I assure you."

"Seems to me that dealing with more than one woman at a time is what would be troubling," Jake responded, inadvertently thinking of Betsy.

"I assure you, those who practice polygamy are only fulfilling the tenets set forth in the Old Testament as they understand them. These men are honorable, by and large, and believe that the practice of polygamy is theologically necessary for salvation."

"Not if that practice means forcing young girls into marrying them."

"That assuredly would never happen. The rumors you've heard are highly exaggerated, trust me."

"Well, I know of one situation for sure," Jake said rising, thinking of Margaret DuBonnet.

"Let me say, then, that forced marriage would be highly irregular." Stillwell smiled and also stood. "Thank you, Marshal Silver, for your time with us this evening. Just having a lawman here greatly reassures our citizenry of our safety and that the outer world has not forgotten us."

"Mr. Stillwell, I wish I could truly grant you the peace of mind that you all seek, but your problems here are far greater than one marshal can attend to. My recommendation is that your community best be thinking of relocating to a more - -" he hesitated, searching for the right word. "A more hospitable area. This is Navajo country, and it rightly belongs to them, as all this land once did."

"Thank you, Marshal, for your advice. We will take it into serious consideration, I assure you, but I trust our relocating will not be necessary. For now, let me show you to your room. It's humble, but you are welcome to stay as long as you wish."

"I'll be on my way tomorrow, Mr. Stillwell. I want to thank you now, in case I'm gone when you awake. I'm an early riser."

"Of course. And you're most welcome. It's been an honor to have you." Stillwell opened a door into a small and sparingly furnished room with only a bed and nightstand, but comfortable nonetheless. An open-paned window looked out into a barren side yard. Beyond the yard stood a barn where his horse was securely stabled. "Windows have not all arrived yet, sorry to say," Stillwell apologized.

"It's no problem," Jake answered.

Knowing he'd rest well now that he didn't have to worry about his horse being stolen, Jake lay back on the feather mattress hoping to drop off to sleep immediately. He'd been traveling and living on the trail for days, and his body yearned for rest, but sleep refused to come. Instead, he thought of Betsy, thankful he'd safely delivered her to Prescott lest she be taken somewhere along the trail and forced into a Mormon household. He knew her sister's fate and wondered if Margaret was adjusting to that way of life. She probably even had a kid or two by now. If she looked at all like Betsy, it would be hard for a man to ignore her. Damn. Here he was thinking about Betsy in that way again, and when he thought about her in that way, it liked to drive him crazy. Maybe there'd be a saloon with women in Freeman. He could only hope.

He arose before dawn after a restless night. Finding Mrs. Stillwell already busy in the kitchen, he thankfully accepted strong, black coffee and a full breakfast.

"I can't tell you what your visit means to us, Marshal Silver. We so seldom get guests here. It's such a pleasure when someone comes by."

"It's been a pleasure for me, too, ma'am. I can't remember when I last enjoyed a dinner so good and a breakfast so fine as last night and this morning."

Mrs. Stillwell smiled, nodding slightly as an acknowledgement of the compliment. "Well, I do hope you'll stop by on your return."

"I wouldn't miss this for a minute. Not sure which route I'll be taking, though. I'm looking to ride down the east side through Navajo country, see if there's any trouble brewing that needs takin' on."

"Well, Marshal Silver, I can only say that you are indeed diligent about your job. Never had a marshal step foot this way. Leastwise, not one that I know of. More coffee?"

"No thanks, Mrs. Stillwell. I best be going. I aim to find the new trading post today. Heard there might be a new one just north of here."

Dawn was just breaking when Jake left the Stillwell ranch and headed north. Despite his horse's eagerness to take off at a dead run, Jake kept the animal to a sitting trot. "Need to get my food digested, Buddy," he explained aloud.

The trail was easy to follow, so Jake spent an hour thinking about the missing girls in Freeman. He'd have to see what the evidence indicated, but it just wasn't the Navajo or the Hopi's nature to commit this kind of crime in times of peace. Despite the high opinion white folk had of themselves, white women were not desirable to all tribes, a few of whom thought of white women as weak, temperamental, and too tearful. He could attest to that. During times of war, however, or when the opportunity presented itself, some tribes captured white women and valued them as slaves or wives. A beautiful woman often gave a warrior who owned her great trading power. Sometimes the owner gambled the captive away. A woman might be traded several times in a gambling session. He couldn't see the Navajos taking the girls, however, no matter which way he thought about it. Doing so wouldn't be worth the risk and the ensuing problems.

Mexicans, on the other hand, might consider a white woman a prize worth taking some risks for. Their male-dominated society took pleasure in fair-skinned, blonde women. Seldom abusive, the Mexican simply hungered for the soft pleasure of a helpless white female.

He eliminated outlaws as the kidnappers. They had women aplenty who found their rough lifestyle and manner irresistible.

In Jake's mind, that left only polygamous Mormons who might swoop in and take the girls. Odds were the girls would not be harmed by their captors. In all likelihood, they'd do their best to convince the young ladies of their coming salvation if they cooperated with the men chosen to be their husbands. Still, it was bad business, even if the girls went along with the notion. Jake knew that not all women took to the idea of sharing a man. The green-eyed monster had gotten the best of every woman he'd ever known, with the exception of Betsy, who seemed largely oblivious to womanly ways.

He shook her from his mind and urged the horse into a faster pace. He wouldn't locate the trading post before dark if he didn't step it up. He planned to spend the night there, then leave for Freeman in the morning. He'd heard the trading post was pretty isolated, but he'd also heard the owner was hospitable to travelers. Jake hoped the man, familiar with the area and its inhabitants, might be a reliable source of information and ideas about the kidnappings.

The horse responded immediately to the slight squeeze of Jake's legs and took off without further encouragement, happily obliging. The two again moved as one, and Jake relaxed into the saddle, relishing the adventure while still keenly aware of his surroundings. He watched particularly for places of likely ambush, but as the way stretched before him almost entirely open he had few concerns.

When he arrived at his destination, Ben McGraw, Kaibito Trading Post owner, greeted him with a hearty handshake and slap on the back. Escorting Jake to the corral securely situated behind the small stone structure out of the line of sight, McGraw talked a steady stream, peppering his monologue with questions about the trip, the territory, and the country.

"Don't get that many white travelers here," he said as he set a large, cast-iron dutch oven over the coals a few yards from the stone structure in which he both lived and traded. "Mostly Indians coming by with hides, stuff like that, pickin' up flour and whatnot. You're lucky you caught me in. I just got back yesterday from Freeman. I been staying there more and more. The town fathers keep predictin' it's gonna grow faster than a stampede, but I got my doubts somehow. But the Indians'r startin' to trade there some now. I'll probably close up here in the next year or two. This particlar location ain't been all that lucrative, tell the truth." The man carried on a monologue for some time, finally running out of steam late in the evening. What Jake heard, however, he found useful.

"So what brings you all the way out here, Marshal?"

"Call me Jake."

"Good to know you're not a stuffed shirt, although when I seen you ride in all dusty and grubby I figured you were a man and not just some dandy wearin' a badge. You out here just to see the sights, or on business?"

"What do you know about the kidnappings happening in Freeman? Anything?"

"Yeah. Figured you might be interested in those. Pity. Young girls taken practically right from under people's noses. Three of 'em so far. Maybe more by now. Last I heard there was three."

"Any ideas?"

"Well, I'll tell you this much, it ain't the Indians. Everybody wants to believe it's Indians. It ain't."

"What makes you so sure?"

"For one thing, I know these Indians. Know 'em better than I do most white folk. They told me they ain't takin' girls. Don't even want 'em. I'm thinkin' it's Mormons from over Utah way."

"I was wondering that myself," Jake said.

"They all wantin' more'n one wife. The pressure's on to scoop up as many as they can before the law gets passed that says they can't have anymore. I got one wife. I'm tellin' you, one's plenty for me. Only two things scare me, and one of em's my wife and she's only a bit of a thing."

Sorely tempted to ask what the other thing was that scared the big, burly mountain man, Jake held back, wondering how long it would take the talkative McGraw to tell. He didn't have to wait long.

"Course the other thing I'm right scared of, and I'm not ashamed to say, is goin' down in that godawful deep canyon. Worst damn trip I ever took. Once yer down there I gotta say it's right amazing, but I can't hardly take that steep descent. Scares the peewad plumb right outta me. Once, I seen half a dozen horses slip and fall over the cliff's edge, and I don't hanker to be on one of 'em. I mostly dismount and walk. Don't care what the other fellas say. That's why I'll be glad to open my trading post in Freeman. I don't like the trip to the canyon bottom to service those people down there. I'll just stay put at my store. Let someone else break their fool neck gettin' down there. I figure if I'm closer to where they are, the folks can come up to me."

"A lot of people down there?"

"You could say so. Mostly Mormon. There's lotsa bad feeling about those folks, but they been fair to me. Pay cash. No squabbles."

The two talked until late, but Jake still walked out back to check on his horse before turning in. The night air made him shiver, and he was glad he'd grabbed a coat. The horse approached, eager for attention, and Jake scratched its forehead and ears. Comforted, the animal moseyed back to a hay crib and Jake turned his attention overhead. He hadn't gazed at the stars in wonder for some years, but thinking of Betsy's unexpected breathless outburst the first night he'd been with her on the trail, gave him pause.

He now looked heavenward and had to admit the indescribable celestial beauty he saw nearly took his breath. He stood for some time looking for constellations, trying to shut her from his memory. He briefly wondered what she'd be doing in Prescott right now. Probably sleeping at this late hour, unless she was attending another gala event in town. Damn. She wasn't gone from his head yet. He returned to the post more determined than ever to forget her once and for all.

Up the Hassayampa

ALMOST overnight Betsy became a celebrity. Her hostess and mentor, Virginia Hall, introduced her widely, and her beguiling story of being sent west on an orphan train and running away into the wild thrilled even the most staid. Her short hair, now grown to a slightly less shaggy length, only added to the dramatic flair with which Betsy learned to tell her tale. She received endless offers of employment and hospitality, and she garnered a great deal of sympathy and admiration for her exploits.

One day Miss Hall engaged a buggy and driver to take her and Betsy to visit a widowed, ailing friend, Ruth Jeffries. One look at the Jeffries' property, and Betsy knew it was the epitome of her dreams, even better than her wildest dreams. It saddened her that Mrs. Jeffries had put the property up for sale, but she could tell that the gentle, sickly owner would probably not live much longer. It pained Betsy to see the beautiful log home, far larger than she'd ever pictured for herself, surrounded by lofty pine, beautiful pastures and tall mountains - - even a stream - - because she knew it could never be hers.

As the days following Jake Silver's departure slowly passed, her thoughts, when not dwelling on him, increasingly reverted to her mother. She'd been told that Wickenburg, where her mother had told her she lived, lie a mere sixty miles away. She remembered Jake's promise of finding her mother as soon as he returned from his current assignment, but as the days wore on she grew impatient. Had he not taught her to survive in the wilds? The route to Wickenburg was a fairly well-traveled route, she'd heard, so she really wouldn't be venturing into the wilds…not really. She could easily get there and back before he returned. Yet, she'd promised to wait and not do anything foolish. Breaking her promise troubled her more than the impending trip she knew she was bound to take. Why did she care about a stupid promise, anyway? she wondered. She'd seen the ladies' heads pivot when he'd made his appearance at the governor's reception. Betsy's insecurities soared when she watched other women, well groomed and attired, devote their attention to the dashing, painfully handsome and eligible Territorial Marshal Jacob Silver.

Each passing day she became increasingly distracted with the idea of heading to Wickenburg. The more she thought about the trip, the more confident she felt. She'd come this far safely, and she had no reason to believe that a final sixty miles would unfold any differently. Maybe she'd just stay with her mother and forget about Jake Silver altogether.

Miss Hall didn't take the news at all well when Betsy told her of her plan to leave. She argued persuasively against the idea, but the more Miss Hall attempted to dissuade her, the more determined Betsy grew. Betsy's happiness began to sour as she thought about her tenuous position, as though the entire town had become her guardian. When she realized that possibly all of them felt sorry for her, thinking of her only as a guttersnipe or an oddity, and that they didn't really admire her bravery and spunk, she left herself no choice but to leave. She had no doubt that her mission would be successful and that she'd be back in Prescott before Jake's return – if she chose to return at all.

Retrieving her trousers, hat, and other riding apparel, she prepared for the journey more thoughtfully than she'd prepared for the journey from Albuquerque. She noticed, however, as she stood before the mirror adjusting her Tom Black ensemble, that a steady diet of nourishing food had changed her boyish figure. She'd have to wear a binder, or a bulky jacket, lest her budding chest betray her true sex. She blushed at the change and wondered if Jake had noticed.

Even though the weather had grown decidedly warmer since the first of June, nights were still cool, so she packed an extra blanket in addition to a bedroll and a jacket. She remembered to borrow hobbles and rope this time, then left at daybreak without saying goodbye to anyone.

Betsy refused to think of obstacles she might encounter, reminding herself that the Indians in the area were largely peaceful. She also had a handgun should a mountain lion or other wild animal come around. She could pass herself off as Tom Black if she encountered anyone along the route. Further, the well-traveled stagecoach route would be so safe, she reasoned, it wouldn't even be like she was doing anything dangerous at all.

The few times that she had misgivings about the wisdom of the trip, pride kept her moving along. She sang quiet songs to Moonlight, thankful that Jake had worked extensively with the horse when they'd been on the trail together. The animal sensed her nervousness, however, and soon began to take advantage of her, as any young horse will.

By evening of the first day, Betsy knew she'd made a terrible mistake by leaving Prescott, but her wounded pride kept thoughts of returning at bay. She vowed she'd never show her face in Prescott again. That would solve everything. Or, if she did return, she'd triumphantly enter town with her mother by her side, so they'd know she'd been successful.

Despite her travels, she'd never before been alone on the trail, and now fear began to stalk her. The first evening she camped well off the route, and as darkness approached she jumped nervously at every sound, her eyes straining to peer into the gathering gloom. Moonlight capitalized on Betsy's uneasiness and became difficult to manage, jerking away from her twice as she tried to secure him for the night. She had to keep control of the horse, no matter what, for without the horse she could die.

"I can do this," she muttered fiercely. "I'm fine. Nothing's wrong. Nothing's gone wrong and nothing will," she repeated loudly as she gathered firewood. She feared being alone in the forest, but she feared someone coming along even more. "Oh God! What have I done?" she gasped, trying to control her growing terror. After a few frantic moments she repeated again, "Nothing's wrong. Absolutely *nothing's* wrong."

She set about making a fire, but after an hour she gave up in disgust and a fit of temper. She'd watched Jake build one nightly for weeks, and he'd made it look incredibly easy. A fire brought so much warmth and security, keeping animals away and making the environment seem more hospitable. But would she have to do without one?

Withdrawing the gun from the saddlebag, only then did she realize that Jake must have removed the bullets. In her haste to pack and to leave, she hadn't taken the time to check her weapon. Now, wrapping herself in blankets, Betsy sat on the cold, hard ground shivering, allowing her tears to flow. She remembered so clearly the night Jake had curled up next to her to warm her. She'd lain in his arms and had never felt so wonderful and secure. She hadn't spoken a word, and it had taken all of her willpower not to wrap her arms about him also. Now, never had she felt so alone. As darkness fully descended, the sounds of the night kept her wide-eyed and on edge, but at some point sleep finally came.

She awoke cold, stiff, and hungry, aware that the patch of sky she could see through the pines was now slate gray and not coal black. Moonlight stood where she'd secured him, and for that she expressed thanks. More than anything she wanted to return to Prescott, but she couldn't. She realized too late that Jake would find out that she'd set out, even if she returned before he did. No choice remained but to forge on. Perhaps today would be better, she thought hopefully.

Once she'd made her way out of the mountain pines, the road flattened some and Moonlight made good progress. Despite her hunger, Betsy pushed on, hoping to reach a settlement of any kind and feeling encouraged when she saw smoke rising in the distance. Late in the afternoon, she forced herself to approach a small cabin to ask if she could camp nearby.

"Lordy, child, what are you doin' out here by yourself?" a matronly woman responded to Tom Black's question. "You just git on down and put that horse up. No young'un should be out here alone. Wash up over there after you're done with the horse then come on in and eat some vittles. You look like you're half starved."

"Thank you so much, ma'am," Tom replied, feeling the familiar weight of worry lift.

The meal of stew and biscuits was simple, but delicious, and Betsy listened to Mrs. Miller prattle on about Indians, crops, the weather, and her husband, whom she expected home any time.

"Why you headin' to Wickenburg, may I ask?" Mrs. Miller took another sip of coffee and eyed her guest curiously.

"Looking for my mother," Betsy replied in her best Tom Black voice.

"How she come to be there?"

"It's a long story, ma'am, and kind of hard to explain. If you don't mind, I'd like to just take my bedroll and lay it out on your porch for the night. I could use a little rest. I didn't sleep much last night in the woods." Betsy smiled, trying not to nod off in the warm room.

"That's just fine. You make yourself comfortable."

"Thank you for the food. I'm truly appreciative."

The woman gathered Betsy's plate and fork. "I don't know who you are, but you're welcome to stay the night," she said in a comforting tone. "Tomorrow my husband can accompany you for a few miles to get you off to a good start. You're some ways yet from Wickenburg. Twenty miles or so from here you'll start descending again. It's a curvy, long, steep descent the stagecoach uses. Be careful. Don't start off in the late afternoon, or you'll run the chance of getting caught part way. Once you're down the mountain, you'll come to a small mining town that has a decent hotel, then it's another fifteen, twenty miles to Wickenburg, but it'll be easier riding."

True to her word, the following morning after breakfast Betsy found Moonlight already saddled and Mr. Miller mounted on his big sorrel. The two rode in silence, Mr. Miller being the taciturn partner of a loquacious spouse. After stopping and giving detailed directions, her host paused a moment. "Young lady, what you're doing is incredibly dangerous. I pray you have a safe conclusion to your journey."

Before she could answer, he wheeled the sorrel about and spurred the horse homeward. Startled, Betsy frowned. So, he'd known…or had he been guessing? What had she done wrong? She'd never lapsed from her Tom Black voice, even once. She thought back to Thomas DuBonnet's advice. Maybe too much smiling and eye contact. Jake had figured her out almost immediately, too. She must do much better to fool the miners in Wickenburg.

Knowing she was somewhere near halfway, having eaten two good meals, and having gotten a good night's sleep, her outlook improved immensely. She rode on, picturing her mother and imagining what they'd say to each other at the moment of their reunion.

Despite her efforts not to think of him, Jake Silver never ventured far from her thoughts, either, and when she allowed herself to envision him, she immediately felt lonely and depressed. She couldn't identify the reason that her stomach fluttered inside whenever she saw him, nor could she explain why she just wanted to stand as close to him as she possibly could - stand so close that their bodies touched. Thinking of him was so pleasing, yet it caused an uneasiness, too. She wondered what it all meant, but the possibilities frightened and embarrassed her, so she refused to ponder them for very long.

The day turned warm, and for the first time in two days she looked about and enjoyed the scenery, always pretending that Jake rode by her side. She continued for a good hour through a magnificent grass-filled mesa, or was it a valley? Jake would know. She let Moonlight graze for an hour while she ate a slab of the thick, heavy bread Mrs. Miller had packed for her. No longer so fearful, she enjoyed the luxury of the wildflowers decorating the grassy valley. In the distance she could see cottonwoods, oaks, pinon pines, and giant granite boulders. She felt very clever knowing the names of trees and rocks. She had Jake to thank for her newfound knowledge.

Horse and wagon tracks now became clearly visible, and the trail grew substantially wider. Cow pies dotted the road from time to time also, and finally, like a great omen, a mule- drawn wagon rolled into sight. She smiled, thankful to be no longer alone or lost. Jake Silver might feel at ease in the wilderness by himself. She did not.

Despite Mrs. Miller's advice and the lateness in the afternoon, Betsy started down the long slope out of Yarnell to Stanton. It had grown cold, cloudy, and windy on Table Top Mountain where the town lie perched, and she didn't relish a night curled up in a tight little ball again, fighting for warmth. Hopefully tomorrow would be her last day on the trail and she'd be in Wickenburg before dark.

The road down Table Top Mountain didn't seem as steep as the route had been two days earlier out of Prescott, nor quite as bad as she'd anticipated. Still, the descent was time consuming. Once off Table Top, the protection offered by the surrounding hills helped block the cold wind. She gave Moonlight a loose rein and let the horse pick his way down the rocky, rough road. Despite her haste, she couldn't help but appreciate the staggering beauty of the jagged landscape. The stage road cut through rugged, rock-strewn hills. Without the road, Betsy doubted one could ride down the steep hillsides, covered almost entirely with sharp rocks and prickly pear cactus.

Three miles down the curvy, coarse passage, the road began to flatten and she expelled a long breath, relieved not to be on the steep part of the rubble-strewn trail, particularly as the sun now hid behind the towering hills on her right. She coaxed Moonlight into a jog until she came to a cluster of cottonwood, indicating the presence of a creek that Mr. Miller had mentioned. A short distance off the road a flat campsite by the burbling stream beckoned, and Betsy couldn't resist. Lush, tall grass grew along the banks of Antelope Creek, something she knew Moonlight needed and would enjoy. She herself would take great pleasure in a good scrubbing in one of the shallow pools. The temperature was decidedly warmer at the base of the mountain, almost hot.

She ate the final piece of Mrs. Miller's bread that night, happy to be out of the cooler high country, and happy to know exactly where she was, but perturbed that she wasn't farther along. She might make Wickenburg tomorrow if the trail didn't give her any more difficult riding, she thought, but she fretted that she might arrive too late in the day to seek out her mother and would have to wait. Nevertheless, her confidence greatly restored, she knew she could camp by herself one last night.

Leaving before sunrise the next morning, Betsy's heart surged with excitement as she rode toward Wickenburg, bypassing Stanton lest more people figure her out. With luck she'd see her mother that very day, and her heart swelled with unspeakable happiness at the thought of finding her. "Remember, no smiling. Don't look people in the eye. Head down. Lower my voice. I'm Tom Black now. Tom Black," she reminded herself many times as she traveled.

Despite her rush, Betsy rode mesmerized through the desert. The desert's heat surprised her, given how cool it had been only the day before. She'd been schooled that deserts were barren, sandy areas where camels and maybe an oasis could be found here and there. What stretched before her now were rolling hills carpeted with saguaro, mesquite, creosote, sage, and other shrubbery she wasn't familiar with. The brown, rocky earth, barely visible beneath the green mantle of wild grass and cacti of every variety, stunned her. She marveled at the desert's magnificence and beauty. Rabbits darted about wildly, and she knew snakes inhabited this terrain also. Hawks filled the air and small lizards scurried before Moonlight's approach. Perhaps this was the area of her dreams, and she tried to picture her little cabin nestled at the foot of a distant hill.

She arrived in Wickenburg by early evening, arousing the curiosity of two local loafers. Frustrated, she heard that Vulture Mine was yet another eight miles or so from the small settlement.

"Who you lookin' for, if I may inquire?" spoke a weathered old man wearing a sombrero and dressed in clothes ready to disintegrate in a puff of wind. His companion eyed her curiously.

"I'm looking for a woman named Marie DuBonnet. She may be married to a man named John Casey."

Both old men looked at each other, then back to her, neither speaking. Finally one of them said, "What's your business with John Casey?"

"I've got no business with Casey," Tom Black answered, spitting for effect. "I'm looking for the woman."

"And what's your business with her, if I may ask?"

Betsy hesitated. Would a man tell a stranger what his business was? She wasn't sure. She tried to picture what Jake would do and realized he'd never let himself be put in the position where he had to answer the questions. She spit again.

"It's personal," she finally responded.

The two old men exchanged another glance.

"It's important," Tom Black added. "It concerns her daughter."

"Bad news, I s'pose?" asked the oldest codger, clearly anxious to hear more.

"It's important I find her."

"Well, she ain't here no more, and neither's John Casey."

"Where are they?" Betsy demanded, her voice involuntarily rising.

"Casey's buried up by the mine. The woman took off with that Limey – Shaun Agar – after he kilt Casey. Not that Casey din't have it comin', mind ya. I never did hanker to a man hittin' a woman, and Casey was mighty heavy handed with that gal. Pretty gal, too, but he beat her up terrible a time or two. Caught her with a little stash o'gold dust the last time and 'bout kilt the poor woman. I guess Agar din't like it even more'n the rest of us and he beat ol' Casey to death."

Betsy stood, shocked and silent, as the morbid story unfolded. Finally she sputtered, forgetting her Tom Black impersonation, "But, what happened to her? Where'd she go?"

"Agar said he'd best get out of town, even though not a person here woulda faulted him fer what he done. He up and asked her if she was wantin' to go with him. She took her few belongin's, climbed aboard the back of Agar's mule, and the two took off. Headed up the Hassayampa," the grimy old man continued. "The man's got claims all over the area and I know he's got one up the river a ways. He's been workin' that claim like the devil hisself."

"How far?"

"What'ya think, Daniel? Ten miles up river?"

"All o' that. Maybe closer to twenty."

"Where's this river?" Betsy asked, anxious to leave immediately.

"Not a river right now, but it's got water in places. Only runs when it rains real good," explained Daniel, casually stroking his straggly beard.

"Just head up the wash. Keep followin' it and you'll find 'em 'ventually. The arroyo winds around. Gets real narrow in a couple spots. His place is on the left, about twenty miles from here. There be a small, flat, elevated patch o' ground, with a draw behind it. Right on the river. I been there once. Watch out if there's any big rains. Those washes run like rivers then, and you don't wanna be in that narrow part if that happens. Right purty ride if you ain't in no hurry."

Betsy mounted quickly while the old man continued to speak.

"There's a good place to camp about four, five miles up. On the left. You'll see big acacias there, *big* trees. Can't miss 'em. 'Most dark now, so you best hurry if you're goin'."

"I tole you before, those ain't acacias, you old fool," Daniel corrected his pal.

"Well, what in the tarnation are they then?"

"I don't rightly know offhand, but I got an ounce o' gold says they ain't acacias."

The two men resumed their sidewalk seats arguing, while Betsy, angered and disappointed, headed Moonlight in the direction the old men had pointed toward. As she rode away she overheard their parting shots:

"Hope that girl finds her mother soon enough," Daniel said as the two watched her ride away.

"She'll be a lot safer up that river than here in town, that's fer sure."

Betsy spurred Moonlight into a lope, intending to ride up the sandy riverbed all night if necessary, but after several miles she realized the foolishness of charging wildly into the dark. Drained from the day's heat, both she and Moonlight needed to stop. Easily locating the camp area the old men had mentioned, Betsy found that the spot made an ideal campsite. A fire pit left by previous campers stood ready for use, and she clapped happily, momentarily forgetting her disappointment, when her efforts to make a fire finally blazed to life. A cooling breeze sprang up after dark, racing up the length of the riverbed. Cottonwoods rustled, and hefty limbs of the giant salt cedars whispered and groaned. It was dark, protected, and surprisingly cool in the camp area. The canopy of limbs overhead grew so thick it was almost roof-like, and what with the soft, sandy ground under her, she felt more secure and comfortable that night than she'd felt since leaving Prescott.

She tried not to think about the horrible events that had happened to her mother, and her own disappointment at not locating her in Wickenburg. She focused instead on the morrow, which she prayed would bring her search to an end. This trip was taking far longer than she'd planned. Jake could be back in Prescott any day, and if he found her gone he'd probably just forget about her in his disgust. Well, that didn't matter. He had more women interested in him than he knew what to do with, and she could never compare to them. They had beautiful dresses. Pretty, long hair. They came from good, wealthy families. She intensely disliked him and them.

She awoke with the dawn. "Today's the day, Moonlight. I can feel it." She rode with resolve, forcing the horse to fully obey her commands. Soon the animal acquiesced and the two moved along swiftly.

"It's got to be ten miles," she muttered. Judging by the sun's height she guessed she'd been traveling for more than two hours. Water flowed now in the riverbed. She couldn't really remember where it'd started. The sand had first appeared damp, then there'd been the tiniest trickle, then suddenly shallow pools formed, and now the water meandered slowly. Moonlight drank greedily, and Betsy waited, remembering to move upstream from the horse before filling her canteen, unlike the first time with Jake when she'd filled downstream, next to the horses.

Had she not been in such a commotion to find her mother, the trip would have been magnificent. Even in her anxiousness, she was keenly aware of the unique character of the area.

The river, more a stream really, flowed snakelike as it meandered between tall, rocky foothills. Sometimes she rode in sand; sometimes rocks lie underfoot. Often she rode on sandbars, even up the stream itself. It was necessary to cross the water repeatedly as the river twisted and wandered in the narrow valley between the surrounding hills. She was surprised at the greenery along the sandy riverbanks. Mesquite appeared in full leaf, and a green, brushy plant lined the waterway. When the breeze calmed, Moonlight violently shook his head and twitched his ears as tiny, annoying insects swarmed the two.

The area was not a canyon exactly, but the rocky, steep hillsides often towered above, looking formidable and utterly impassable. Sometimes only fifty feet stretched between the walls of rock on either side of the river; at other times the distance was much greater. Piles of debris lying along the banks indicated that the water could rise much higher and run more swiftly. Still, the gurgling of the now shallow stream as it flowed over river rock was melodious and relaxing. She'd never seen so many large cacti, almost a forest of them, lifting their beefy arms skyward. That some of them seemed to grow out of the rocks amazed her. It was beautiful. More than beautiful. It was magnificent.

Jere D. James

The hot, humid air along the river caused her to stop briefly and rest. She hoped that Shaun Agar hadn't skipped out and taken her mother with him. She'd seen no sign of human life, other than what looked like some tracks occasionally emerging from the water. She reclined against a flat rock in the shade of a mesquite, while Moonlight contentedly munched on wild grass. She wondered if the reason she'd slowed was simply to postpone more disappointment should her mother and the man not be found up this river.

Suddenly, a sharp sound snapped and echoed, like the distant crack of a rifle. Simultaneously, both her and Moonlight's heads jerked up. Several more cracks reverberated off the canyon walls, and her heart began to beat rapidly. Fear compelled her to hide, and she pulled Moonlight from the ankle-deep water up a sandy bank to a heavily treed, brushy area. Her instincts proved right, for within a few minutes a man riding a white horse galloped full tilt down the riverbed, water flying. Peeping cautiously through the bushes, expecting to see more men following him

175

either in pursuit or escape, she caught a glimpse of the fleeing rider. Moments later another horse fled downstream with its rider slumped over, barely hanging on.

Her mind flooded with questions that left worry in their wake. Should she continue? Go back? Once again she found herself profoundly wishing that she'd never left Prescott. This was all a horrible, horrible mistake on her part. Intuitively knowing that the search for her mother was doomed, she remounted, continuing on only because she didn't know what else to do.

Finally, she edged around a bend and there it was, exactly as the old men had described - a flat, raised area by the river with a draw running behind it. A tent sat pitched near a fire pit. Clothes lay strewn along the riverbank, which she thought odd, and then she saw a body, face down in the shallow water, blonde hair floating on the water's surface. Betsy's cry of despair echoed off the canyon walls.

Freeman

JAKE Silver approached the small settlement of Freeman after a relatively short day's ride over a desolate, sandy, windswept route from the trading post. For a tiny town, Freeman looked to have big ambitions, as most of the buildings were uncommonly large, as if the town folk anticipated rapid growth. A few of the buildings stood two stories, the bottom floors built of stone and adobe, while the upper levels were constructed of wood. Only two streets wide, the town measured less than a quarter mile square. A few people walked along wooden boardwalks going about their daily business, but only a handful of horses stood tied at hitching posts. A striking black-and-white paint caught Jake's eye as he rode by, but the .50 caliber Sharps buffalo rifle on the saddle attracted him even more.

He stopped at Charles Caspar's office, a small, square, one-story structure near the end of the main street, where the sheriff greeted him like a long-lost friend. The heavyset Caspar wore a worried look.

"I heard you were headed this way. Can't tell you how pleased I am to have you here. Things are sure not as they should be, let me tell you that right off."

"Yeah, heard all the way in Prescott that you've had some kidnappings."

"Worse than kidnappings, Marshal. They're bad enough, but we've had a string of murders to go along with them.

Jake's attention ratcheted up a notch. "Really? No one mentioned any murders. What's going on?"

"Not sure, to be honest. There's been five attacks overall. Every single person killed. Three girls abducted."

"If everyone's been killed, how do you know there's been abductions?"

"Most of the folks involved were local, or ones that stopped in town for supplies. Some of the folks around here have given up on the area and are movin' on. Don't know how many more been killed that we don't know about."

"Got any leads?"

"None. Locals are thinking it's Indians. But that just don't feel right."

"That's what I've heard from others, too."

"I hate to say it, but I'm beginning to wonder if it's not the Mormons livin' down in that canyon. They don't take to intruders, and let's face it, they're secretive and got a bloody past."

"But what would be the motive?" Jake asked, perplexed.

"You tell me, Marshal. This just don't make no sense at all. None of it. It's plumb crazy."

"So, who are the missing girls?"

"Like I said, there's three that we know of. We got Patsy Baker, Victoria Galloway, and Susie Gatch," he said, reading their names off a slip of paper. "Range in age from thirteen to fifteen.

Those are the ones we know about. Could be more."

"What about the killings?"

"Well, it's clear that every one of these groups was ambushed and shot, that's for certain. Sometimes their wagons were set on fire and we just find charred remains, but we never find any of 'em in any sort of defensive posture. It's like they don't see it coming. 'Course, horses and livestock are always missing. Things look looted. You know, just tossed about. Makes no sense unless you think it's Indians that done it, but I'm telling you it ain't Indians. They been real peaceful and puttin' up with white folks livin' in their territory. 'Course, they're makin' money from it, but still...."

"Anybody here stand to prosper by these murders?" Jake asked, wondering if there was a plot afoot to make money from some bloody scheme.

"Don't know of anyone. There's no wills bein' made out before these folks die. There's no land worth much, although what comes on the market is usually bought up for a few cents on the dollar by that speculator, William Eliot and his partner Clifford Bell. No crime in that really. Eliot's right open about bein' a 'spec'lator. Bell's an attorney. Eliot uses Bell to draw up the paperwork and deeds. Never looked into their business much myself."

"Let me ask you, what's the status of this community? Growing? Prospering?"

"Tell you the truth, we've had some problems. Water's a big issue. Climate ain't been so friendly, either. The only people prosperin' are the Mormons and the Indians, and they live in the canyon. Prime real estate down there but, of course, untouchable for outsiders. Lots of resentment about that. After the Indians, the Mormons settled here first, though. Whatcha gonna do? The whole damn place really belongs to the Indians if you want to know my go-to-hell opinion."

Jake smiled and nodded. He understood all too well and shared the sheriff's unpopular sentiment. It often sickened him when he thought about the injustice done to the indigenous natives of the country. White man's greed had no equal, and he was now wondering what role greed might have played in the deaths and kidnappings of these settlers.

"I think I'll go get a room at the hotel and then head out that way tomorrow," Jake said.

"I'll go with you out to the canyon, if you don't mind a little company."

"Sounds good. Let's leave early. First light. Meanwhile, I'd like to meet some of the town's key players, starting with Bell and, what did you say the speculator's name was?"

"William Eliot."

"Bell and Eliot."

"Bell's office is about four doors down. Eliot keeps a desk over at the bank. Might wanna meet with Robert Pendert, too. He owns the bank. Handles Eliot's financial transactions. You thinkin'- -?"

"I'm not sure what I'm thinking yet. I just know I don't think it's Indians," Jake said as he stood to leave.

"I'll see you in the morning then, Marshal. You got any questions or run into any problems, I'm here to help any way I can."

"Thanks, Charles. Much obliged."

Jake untied his horse and walked slowly down the street toward the hotel. Besides wanting to get a layout of the town, he wanted to get a good look at the black-and-white paint carrying the Sharps. He'd meant to ask the sheriff about the owner of the horse and rifle. He'd do that if he ran into him again, or at least he'd make a note to ask tomorrow.

The paint still stood before the law office. Well, now, he'd have to make a visit sooner than later. First, however, he decided to get a room and clean up. Days on the trail had left their mark.

***

Clifford Bell, attorney at law, paced the cramped office, running a sweaty hand through his thinning hair. Peering anxiously over the top of his glasses, he watched William Eliot and Frank Fernley lounge insolently about his office, obviously taking pleasure in his anxiety.

"I'm telling you, this man frightens me," Bell repeated. "I don't think we should take this marshal lightly. Trust me in this. I've seen him. You haven't. Just wait until you do."

"Now, Clifford, you're panicking over nothing," Eliot said, a smirk evident on his pink, puffy lips. "He's just a lawman. They can all be bought -- or killed. He knows nothing and never will. Relax."

"We didn't plan on the law coming all the way out here from Prescott, William," Bell said, his voice quivering. "You promised that would never happen. If I'd have known this would come to pass, I'd have never stood for Fernley here and his boys taking those young girls. It's got to stop, and I mean it."

"Or what?" dared Frank Fernley. "What're you gonna do about it? Sue me? Ha ha ha." Fernley's manner and tone bespoke violence and evil. Bell shuddered when he thought of the indignities the girls must be suffering at the hands of this miscreant and his gun slinging pals. How had things come to this? The plan had been so clean and simple when he and Eliot had first conceived it. Eliot had reassured him that he knew just the right men for the job.

"Let's be reasonable here," Eliot finally broke in. "It's very simple. Our plan is working, that's the most important thing to remember. Fernley and his boys have only got a few more incidents to pull off and the land will be ours for the taking. You'll feel better when the money starts rollin' in, Cliff."

"But I'm worried about this marshal that's showed up. I'm telling you, he won't just look the other way or give up. He's got that look about him."

"Hey! We can take care of him, so shut your trap. It's three against one," Fernley spat. "He doesn't know about us, and he won't be suspecting. It'll be easy pickings."

"I just don't want to take part in a plan that gets a U.S. Deputy Marshal killed," Bell said, trying not to whine. "I'm supposed to be upholding the law, for Christ's sake."

"You weren't so interested in upholding the law when we first talked about this enterprise," Eliot interjected. "Now you're getting all holy on us. Not a good way to treat your business associates, Cliff. Makes me worried you're gonna turn tail on us."

"Now, don't go making those accusations, William."

"Not accusing, Cliff. Just getting mighty suspicious and concerned about you."

"You know I'm in this the whole way," Bell sputtered. "It's just that I wish I'd been consulted before the boys decided to start taking hostages and, well, I suspect they're abusing those young girls."

At this Fernley burst into guffaws. "Man's gotta have a few pleasures, what with livin' in a cave all these weeks, eatin' beans and shootin' strangers." He paused for effect, then added, "Them's nice, innocent girls, too. More fun than a whole passel of whores, let me tell ya."

Bell cringed. "It's got to stop," he said, now pleading with Eliot. "No more. Enough people have been killed. Things will swing our way without further interference by Mr. Fernley and friends."

"I'll make that determination when I think it's time," Eliot responded. "You just sit here and shuffle your papers and keep your trap closed. You'll thank me later."

Suddenly the door to Bell's one-room office opened. "Sorry. Didn't know you were busy. I'll come back," the imposing man wearing a marshal's badge said, scanning the occupants of the room before turning to leave.

"No. By all means, do come in," Eliot responded, slyly winking at Bell and Fernley. "We were just discussing the sorry state of affairs regarding the disappearance of the young girls and the massacre of the travelers. What a terrible shame."

"And you are…?" the stranger asked.

"I'm William Eliot, a land speculator. This is Clifford Bell, attorney, and that's Frank Fernley."

The tall man nodded. "Pleasure. Jake Silver. U.S. Deputy Marshal. So, what's your interest in all of this, Mr. Eliot?" Silver asked.

"Just good business, Marshal, not to have dead folk and kidnappings going on. Here I am trying to attract newcomers to buy land in Freeman, but it's a hard sell when we got these problems."

Bell felt the marshal's sharp assessment of them. An uncomfortable pause ensued, and Bell was about to say anything just to break the unnatural silence when the marshal turned to Fernley.

"And you, Mr. Fernley, what's your interest in these goings on?"

Fernley's face, a study in disrespect, twisted into a sinister grin. "Just bein' a good citizen, Marshal. Brotherly love and all that."

Quickly Bell cleared his throat in a pathetic attempt to distract the marshal. "So, you've visited with Sheriff Caspar already?"

"Saw him a bit ago."

Bell hoped that more information would be forthcoming, but when the marshal said nothing further, a deepening silence again blanketed the room. Only Fernley, wearing a snide grin, seemed to be enjoying the tension.

"I'll come back later, Mr. Bell," Silver said.

"No, please stay. We were just leaving," William Eliot said as he stood and motioned for Fernley to do likewise. "Clifford, I trust you will keep matters in hand regarding our mutual business."

"Of course. Have no worries. Thank you for stopping by. Good day to you both."

Neither man spoke for a moment after the office door closed, then Silver commented nonchalantly, "Interesting friends for an attorney to keep."

Bell looked up nervously. "Excuse me? What does that mean?"

"Means, Mr. Bell, that at least one of your friends is a felon. Recognized him right off. Frank Fernley. I'll have to attend to him before I leave."

Bell felt a sickening lurch in his stomach. "He's not my friend, I assure you. He's an associate of Mr. Eliot's." Why had he not checked out Fernley and his henchmen before he'd agreed to use their services? "Now, how can I help you today, Marshal?"

"I believe you already have, Mr. Bell. Have a pleasant day."

After the marshal left, Clifford Bell's heart raced in fear. He'd been right about the lawman. Perhaps he should pack up and leave town instantly. But no sooner had the thought entered his mind than he realized the plan's futility. He'd not make it five miles before he'd be hunted down by the likes of Fernley. How had things come to such an unsavory muddle? It'd been so simple in the beginning. As far as he was concerned, the goal had been to get the Mormons to move on so he and Eliot could buy up the canyon lands at a cheap price, carve out large portions for themselves, then sell the rest at an exorbitant price. Once people knew there was gold to be found in the canyon, the rush would be on. The town of Freeman would never survive without the bounty from the canyon. Dusty, dirty, windy, and dry, crops withered in the baking heat of the summer and froze in the frigid temperatures of the winter. Water was scare up on the high land, but at the bottom of the canyon water freely flowed, timber grew thick, wildlife thrived, grassland could easily be cultivated, and climate remained temperate most of the year. To top it off, gold had been discovered in the canyon by a crusty old miner, Old Moses Malone. Malone hadn't lived long enough to tell anyone about his find after scurrying into Bell's office wanting to stake a claim on someone else's private property, madder than hell that the Mormons owned it. Bell refused to think about his own complicity when the man simply disappeared after Bell mentioned Malone and his find to Eliot. Money lay waiting to be had, pure and simple. The Mormons must be driven out.

He hadn't planned on there being any murders, but Eliot and Fernley hatched the idea to rob and kill travelers passing through, making it look like the work of fanatical Mormons. That was Fernley's reason for taking the girls. "Mormons need lots'a wives," he'd said. The goal was to rile the local townspeople to the point where they went after the Mormons. Neither Bell nor Eliot had counted on the locals blaming the Indians instead. Bell could see now that the whole plan had been too hastily hatched, ill conceived, and poorly executed. Everything sounded completely illogical when he thought about it. What had he been thinking? If it wasn't for the Mormons, the town of Freeman would already have failed. Their commerce kept local businesses going and Freeman thriving. What had he done?

Now, a U.S. Deputy Marshal had entered the fray. Bell intuitively knew this marshal would not simply wander off without getting to the bottom of things. He opened his desk drawer and retrieved a small caliber handgun. Before he could make a decision, however, a hullabaloo arose in front of the sheriff's office.

Shaun Agar

THE Irishman lowered his rifle at the sound of the girl's cry. He hadn't recognized the horse or rider, and after the ambush he wasn't willing to take any chances. Despite his pain, he lay silently watching while the girl slid from her horse and ran, stumbling, through the shallow stream. One look at the blonde hair as she tore off her black hat and he knew instantly that the girl was Marie's daughter. Which one he didn't know, but there was no mistaking.

Her cries rent the air and caused tears of his own to well. The loss of Marie pained him far more than the bullets embedded in his body. The girl gently turned the woman over and pulled her onto the sandy beach. Weeping, she knelt, holding the dead woman in her arms. He could hear her clearly call her mama. After some minutes the girl gently laid his dead Marie down on the sandy beach and stood, vacantly looking about for the horse. Finding it, she led it up the embankment to the campsite where she tethered it to a cottonwood.

"Help me. Over here," Shaun weakly called to her. He lay sprawled and bleeding on the ground.

Startled, the girl turned.

"Lassie, I'm glad you're here. I'm sorry about your ma," Shaun said in short gasps, pain squeezing his chest. "Can you help me to the tent before I bleed to death in the dirt?" As the girl warily approached, he looked into her tear-streaked face and winced as he saw Marie's crystal blue eyes peering at him.

"I'll try," she said the moment she realized he was incapable of harming her. "How should I do it?"

"Pull my left arm. I got one good leg I can push with. It's not far, lass. You can do it."

Each tug caused blood to ooze and Shaun to grimace.

"I should go for help," she said, appalled by the thick trail of blood spread along the hard packed dirt.

"There's no time. I'll be dead before you return. You'll have to help me."

"I… I don't know what to do!" she exclaimed, her eyes widening.

"I can tell ya, coax you through it."

"No, I can't do it. You've been shot! At least twice!"

"Lass, you must help me, or you'll watch me die! I got to tell you before I pass out here. Now, listen sharp!" He felt his life energy abandoning him, and he spoke in short gasps.

Haltingly he gave the girl directions on sterilizing the knife in the remaining coals in the fire pit, slicing the bullet holes wider if needed, putting her fingers into the openings to pull the loads out, and using the tip of the knife to help if necessary. "Pour some old orchard on it after, but give me a swig right now and save some to dull the pain later."

"This, this is a surgery. I - -" again she protested.

"Lass, your mother'd be 'shamed to see that her daughter's such a weakling. Buck up now and help me, dammit! Do as I say. I been shot worse before and lived to tell of it," he finished breathlessly.

***

Once on the cot, Agar turned ashen. Betsy figured a fair complexion was probably his Irish trademark, but his pale face now looked deathly. Along with an unruly mop of long, curly red hair, at least a two-day's growth of beard made the injured man look otherwise tough. He was not large, perhaps only five foot seven or eight, but his body looked sinewy and hard.

Betsy counted two wounds, one in his side and another in his thigh. She'd never seen so much blood and felt sick to her stomach when she looked at the seeping holes. Glancing about the tent, she spied a small table cluttered with tools, bullets, and other paraphernalia. She finally found the dirty, bone-handled knife in a scabbard on his belt.

Agar screamed and fell unconscious as Betsy used the hot knife to slice into him. She gagged as the skin separated under the sharp blade. Rinsing her fingers in water that she found in a teapot, she proceeded to gingerly probe the wounds, gagging all the while. The bullet from his side was shallow, and she removed it easily enough, silently congratulating herself. The second took deeper probing and digging which caused her to gag and grimace even more. Since the bullet had lodged in his thigh, she consoled herself that at least no vital organs would be damaged by her amateur explorations.

She poured a small amount of whiskey over the wounds as he'd directed, then tearing strips from a wool blanket, she fashioned a dressing as best she could. She took up the bottle of whiskey and swallowed a sip, hoping it would calm her nerves. Never having tasted spirits before, she choked as the burning liquid scorched her throat. Looking at her handiwork, she saw the makeshift dressing on his thigh quickly saturating with blood.

"I need a needle and thread," she said in dismay. Rummaging through a basket of notions on the table, she found what she was looking for. Faint and nauseated when she stuck the needle through the man's skin, she tugged the thread through to the other side, choking back whiskey-laden bile which burned her throat worse than when it'd gone down.

Finally, she knew could do no more, and she left the tent to wash her sticky hands in the stream and to stand vigil by her mother.

She sat for some hours, holding her mother's hand, singing softly, reflecting on their past together, her belated search, and now her overwhelming sorrow. Finally, wiping away her tears, she sighed deeply. Somewhere the man would have a shovel.

Three days passed before Shaun Agar awoke, burning with fever. At first his mumblings revealed he thought the "angel" beside him was his beloved Marie. "Water, Marie, I need water."

Lifting his head, Betsy tried to give him a sip, most of which ran down his neck. He smiled weakly in appreciation, closed his eyes, and didn't awaken for another two days.

On the fifth day, Betsy sensed him watching her as she moved about the fire pit. She'd tied back the tent's flaps, allowing the cool morning river breeze to blow in.

"Miss. Could you come, please?"

"You're awake! I've been so worried about you! How are you feeling?"

"I think I'll live, by golly." He paused to catch his breath. "Are you Betsy or Maggie?"

"I'm Betsy. You must be the Shaun that I heard about?"

"The same. Shaun Agar of Killarney. At your service." He paused, momentarily overcome by lightheadedness. "Well, soon at your service. I thought you might be Betsy by your mother's description."

"Your fever seems to be gone, but you look so white. Why don't you just rest? I've made some food. It's not very good, but it might help you get some strength back. You need to get well 'cause I've got to be leaving."

"You're an angel for sure, Betsy. Some water first, then a bit o' food."

Betsy saw by the look on his face that he silently agreed the food wasn't very appetizing, but he ate a bit, telling her that too much could be bad. He slept again and didn't awaken until the next morning.

"If you can get me a big, strong limb, I can fashion myself a crutch," he said. "How long have I been under?"

Betsy thought a bit, counting back, trying to keep track of the days. "Five, no maybe six days from the day I came. You've slept an awful lot. I thought you'd never wake up."

"Ah! Sleep is the body's time to mend itself." He sat, grimacing and woozy with pain, but finally able to swing his legs to the side of the bed. "We should talk, I reckon. But first, the limb. I'd feel better mendin' out in the sunshine. People die in bed, as my grandmother used to say."

Betsy hauled several large branches before the Irishman chose the one he wanted. She retrieved a hatchet from the woodpile and the still bloody knife from the table for him, and the ailing man began to chop and whittle as much as his strength allowed. He gave Betsy discreet directions on how to prepare a broth with beans, hoping some food would revive his strength. He also told her that despite the loss of Marie, when he looked out at the blue sky and the meandering little stream, he felt glorious to be alive.

By the next afternoon he'd fashioned a crutch out of the long limb, and with Betsy's assistance he hobbled outside to sit in the afternoon sun. He continued to direct her cooking efforts, amused at her ineptitude. "What we need is a nice rabbit stew. Whyn't you take the rifle and fetch us a rabbit?"

"I - - I've never shot a rifle before," Betsy confessed, amazed that he would make such a request.

"Why, your mother was a crack shot, let me tell you. She could hit a rabbit's arse from fifty feet, make that a hundred feet, I swear."

"Mother shot a gun and killed rabbits?" she stammered, shocked.

"She kilt more than rabbits, lass. She kilt deer, an antelope once, and even shot a steer that wandered by the camp."

"Where'd she learn to shoot?"

"Why I taught her! I'll teach you too, how's that? But, you mean to be tellin' me that you rode in here not packing any weaponry?"

"Well, I have a little gun, but no bullets. Someone took 'em from me."

"What a dirty trick to play."

"Oh, he was just trying to protect me, in his way."

"Ha! Now you're defending the lowdown dog who took your ammunition. You must be sweet on him."

Before Betsy could answer he said, "Bring me the rifle inside the tent. The Henry."

It took two trips before Betsy finally retrieved the right weapon. Shaun carefully showed her how to load it, hold it, aim, and fire. He watched her clumsily repeat his movements which he said reminded him of Marie's first pathetic attempts. A few rounds later, however, Betsy's aim improved considerably and her confidence with the weapon grew.

***

"Go fetch a rabbit, lass, but don't go far. Don't shoot in this direction, either," he yelled as an afterthought as she forded the stream. He watched her turn and smile, and his heart broke. The girl was a spittin' image of his Marie, and it pained him to see her, yet pleasured him also.

There was no rabbit stew for dinner, but Shaun gave Betsy assurances that it was only a temporary deprivation for them.

"We've some things to talk about, Betsy," he said as the two quietly sat by the fire in the growing dark. "No point in avoiding. I'm sure you got your questions, and I got mine."

"Well, one thing I've got to say is that I've got to get going. I've really got to get back to Prescott just as soon as you can tend to yourself."

"Soon, Betsy. Just be a mite patient. But I'm meanin' other things we need to talk about."

"Like what?" she asked simply, but Shaun detected the tone, the same her mother used that indicated she well knew where the conversation would head.

"How'd you come to be here?"

"I don't even know where to begin. It seems it all began so long ago." She paused for a few moments and ran her fingers through her hair while he patiently waited.

She began describing what had happened to her, and the story took some time. Shaun listened patiently and recognized that when the narrative involved the lawman, her emotions ran much higher than when she related the rest of the tale.

"I ran out of most of my money, though, and had to get off in Albuquerque where Thomas helped me buy my horse. Then this lawman kind of," she paused again, "this lawman came to my rescue, sort of. He took me to Prescott. I was supposed to wait there until he came back from a business trip to Freeman. He promised he'd look for Mama then, but I got to thinking about her and got impatient and, well, here I am."

Shaun sat for some minutes, studying the fire and then her. "I suppose there's more to your story, but that'll do for now. Unless you're wantin' to tell me about the lawman, of course."

He could tell by her hesitation that there was more to the story. Even in the low light of the fire he could see her expression of dismay.

"Not much to say, really. He was kind and helpful. He..." Her voice trailed off.

"So, you're a bit soft on him, is that what you're sayin'?"

"Oh, no. I... I..."

He watched emotions dance across her delicate face. "A lawman's a good man to get attached to. No shame in that. Better a lawman than a miner," he said in an effort to add levity to the moment.

"I could never be attached to Jake Silver. He's just, well, he's just grander than life, I suppose. He'd never notice the likes of me. Not with all the highfalutin Prescott women having a mind to flirt with him."

"Land sakes, lass! Don't be sellin' yourself short. You're a beauty, just like your mama was."

"Tell me about her."

"Betsy, she was the finest woman I ever had the pleasure to know. Beautiful on the outside, but even more beautiful on the inside." His voice cracked with emotion, and it was some minutes before he collected himself. Finally he continued, "She talked about you girls all the time. I heard her prayin' every night. I give her a bag of gold dust to pay for your trip out here from New York, but I guess you'd already left by the time it got there. Then a month or so ago a letter finally arrived. It said that you'd been placed with a nice family in Iowa. Your mama cried for a week and swore she'd find you. I told her she could have every double eagle I owned to go get you, but I told her there wasn't no use runnin' around an entire state looking for one girl. She wrote again askin' where they placed you. We were gonna mail the letter the next time we went to town."

"How'd she die? What happened here?" Betsy asked, her voice low and husky.

"Claim jumpers. I've been attacked before, but this time was different. I took a large poke into the bank a few days ago. I'm thinkin' they must've seen me." He paused, the memory of the attack bringing a mixture of anger and sorrow to his eyes. "Marie got up that mornin' lookin' so beautiful and smilin', as always. Said she was gonna wash out some clothes since it looked like good weather." He chuckled and added, "That woman washed clothes more'n any woman ever. Anyway, I said okay and warned her to be watchin' for rattlers. They're comin' out now that the weather's warmin'. I heard her singin' and then I heard her yellin', 'Shaun, someone's coming.' Next I heard a rifle fire." Stirring the embers, he tossed more wood on the dying fire and said nothing further for some moments. "I got one of 'em. I don't think he made it far. The other took off back down river."

"I saw them," Betsy said. "I was hiding in the bushes when they went by."

"I been wantin' to ask, Betsy. Where'd you put your mama?"

"She's up there," Betsy nodded her head in the direction, "by the cottonwood grove. It took me two days to dig her grave. I laid her in my wool blanket. Put lots of rocks on top. I was going to show you before I left."

Both sat silent for some minutes watching the fire's glow and listening to the gurgling stream. Finally, Betsy spoke, "I gotta be going, Shaun. You know that. You're well now and you'll be okay."

"You can't leave now, Betsy. I'm still in a bad way. Stay just a bit longer, lass. When I can walk enough to get on the mule, you can leave. Besides, the rains are comin'. Can't you feel 'em?"

"I have to go back to Prescott," she answered with more insistence than he'd seen from her before. "I've got to get back before Jake returns! I've been gone so much longer than I planned."

"Betsy, it ain't safe to travel on horseback in the rains. The washes roar with water and become raging rivers. It's gonna rain before tomorrow. You'll see."

"How can you tell? Look! The stars are out! There's not a cloud in the sky!"

"Smell the air. It's in the air, Betsy. Feel it. The air's heavy and slow. I saw big thunder clouds gathered today along the canyon rim. You'll see tomorrow."

As though orchestrated, suddenly a brilliant flash of lightning and a loud peal of thunder rumbled the length of the canyon, reverberating off the rock walls. A moment later the wind picked up, and the flaps of the tent beat in the air.

"We best go inside for the night, lass. It's goin' to rain sooner than I expected."

The storm was unlike anything the girl had ever experienced, and Shaun watched her quiver when flashes of lightning lit the sky. Thunder boomed so loudly she covered her ears and screamed.

Soon, both of them could hear the water rising as the rain poured down heavily, swept sideways at times by the frantic wind. Betsy cried, and Shaun knew it was not the storm that drove her to tears, but her disappointment in not being able to return to Prescott to see her lawman.

Every day for two weeks the storms arrived in the late afternoon or early evening and the tiny Hassayampa River overran its lower banks. Moonlight and Shaun's mule, bound in friendship by a makeshift corral comprised of cottonwoods, old wire, and cactus ribs, turned their hind ends to the wind and rain, looking pitiful in their soggy pen. The fire had to be relit every day, and finding dry kindling became the biggest chore of the day. Twice Betsy returned from her short outings with a rabbit, however, and the smile on her face warmed Shaun's heart.

The two played cards, told stories, and talked about their pasts. Shaun's past was far more colorful and adventurous than Betsy's, and to his delight he kept her enthralled for hours at a time with his blarney and tales of ocean voyages and journeys to distant lands. He told her he'd met Kit Carson, Wild Bill Hickok, Buffalo Bill Cody, Wyatt Earp, and a host of other Western characters. Since Betsy claimed she'd never heard of any of them, Shaun knew he had a willing, gullible audience.

"Do all Irishmen have red hair?" Betsy asked one evening while he was teaching her to play poker.

"Only the ones who've kissed the Blarney Stone," he answered proudly. "When a person kisses the blarney stone, it means they'll always have the gift of gab. And, of course, red hair," he added hastily.

"Really?"

"I swan, 'tis true. And I'm a wee bit shorter than most of my countrymen, but I've got the mean Irish temper."

"Is that why you killed that man? John Casey in Wickenburg?"

Shaun remained silent while he reshuffled the cards. "I killed that man because I loathed the way he treated your mother. I'll be honest with you,

Betsy. I was in love with your mama the first day I laid my green eyes on her. John Casey was a rambunctious scalawag and not deservin' of that beautiful, fine woman. He did her wrong in my presence, and I sent him to eternal hellfire where he belonged."

"I heard he beat her. Is that true?"

"I can't lie to you, lass. 'Tis true."

Both sat for some minutes while Shaun continued shuffling the deck, mindless of how many times he did so.

Finally Betsy broke the silence. "How long will the rains last, Shaun? I must go back to Prescott. I'm sure Jake's back by now. He'll be so angry with me. I promised him, I *swore an oath* to him," she added with emphasis, "that I'd not leave."

"The rains can last another month or two. Usually there's a break in them, though. This be a long spell we're havin' right now."

He watched her carefully and knew her mind was not on her cards. "Look, Betsy, as soon as it's safe, I'll take you to Prescott myself."

"No. I was just thinkin', it's silly of me to go back anyway. He won't want to see me. I don't know why I'm so worried about it. It was probably the happiest day of his life when he got me safely to Prescott and could finally wash his hands of me."

"So, where will you go, if not back to Prescott?"

"I'll find Margaret!" she exclaimed, as though a new sun had risen on the horizon.

"Do you know where she is?"

"I know she's married to a Mormon. That's what she wrote in her letter. I know I can find her, Shaun. I just *know* it! I found mama, didn't I?"

"Now that's a scary proposition, lass. If you're not careful, you'll find yourself a Mormon prisoner and wife in one of their harems."

"I'll go as Tom Black. No one will know I'm a girl."

"I doubt that," he said, trying not to chuckle at the thought. "Show me then, your Tom Black self."

Betsy pulled the black hat low over her brow, turned up her collar, and stood, legs apart, arms crossed over her chest. "Lookin' for a Margaret DuBonnet," she said in her low, surly Tom Black voice.

"Tell me when you're ready, now, so I'll know your bein' Tom Black," he said, laughing so hard his face turned red and his voice disappeared. His gales of laughter caused tears to stream down his face.

Betsy scowled good-naturedly and tossed the hat on her cot. "I'm leaving when the rains stop, Shaun. And I'm going after Margaret. She's all, absolutely all, that I have left," she said in a serious tone.

Into the Canyon

APPEARING out of nowhere, a small mob of people stood along the boardwalk, spilling into the dusty street. Heated barbs blasted forth as men swore and shook their fists. Women clutched their chests as though in mortal fear. Jake pushed his way through the fiery crowd and entered the sheriff's cubicle of an office.

Before him lay the battered body of a half-clad girl. Broken and bloodied, the corpse bore deep bruising, severe head wounds, twisted joints, and broken bones.

"Found her this morning, sheriff, lying at the foot of Diablo Peak all crumpled up in the rocks. Looks like she fell – or jumped."

Charles Caspar looked up, clearly relieved that Jake Silver now stood in the doorway, surveying the scene. "Come on in, Marshal, and shut the door behind ya."

"What's going on?" Jake asked, scrutinizing the tall, impressive   man standing before the sheriff. Clean shaven, well dressed and groomed, the man's composure indicated utter self-confidence.

"Jake, this is Jeremiah Atkins. He's a Mormon who lives in the canyon. Says he found this girl on his way up to Freeman this morning."

Jake didn't doubt for a minute the veracity of the man's story. The only way the girl could have sustained such injuries was if she'd fallen from a great height, or from a beating he could not begin to imagine. "Do you know who she is, Tom?"

"Yes. 'Fraid I do. It's Susie Gatch. No question about it."

A moment of silence passed before Jake spoke. "I think we'd best detail the extent of her injuries. For the record. You want to write the information down, Charles?"

"Yes. Of course." The sheriff seemed older than when Jake had seen him only a brief time ago. He stood stooped, as though he could carry no more.

Methodically, Jake inspected and detailed the girl's massive external injuries while Caspar took careful notes. Jeremiah Atkins stood quietly, head bowed as though in prayer.

Jake guessed that nearly every bone in the young girl's body had been broken, many savagely piercing through her skin. He strongly suspected she'd also been raped, but he refrained from stating what the two other men would obviously also surmise.

Atkins recounted in detail his journey that morning and how he'd found the girl. "If it hadn't been for the buzzards circling I'd have paid no mind. Fortunately, I found her before they could do their work."

"Since I see no sign of any kind of decomposition or buzzard or coyote damage, I'm guessing you came upon her very shortly after her…fall," Jake concluded.

"I suspect you're right, Marshal. But what would induce a young girl to do such a thing?" Atkins asked, shaking his head in sorrow.

"Oh, I can think of a few things," Jake said, stifling his growing anger as he remembered the brutal aftermath of several rapes he'd investigated while still a lawman in Kansas. Turning to Caspar he said, "Sheriff, I think you need to deal with the small group of rabble rousers outside. Calm people down. We don't need for Mr. Atkins to be lynched."

Caspar nodded and stepped outside the office. Instantly the crowd besieged him with questions and demands for justice.

"I'd like you to come with me tomorrow," Jake said. "I want to see where you found this girl. I'd also like to see the canyon I keep hearing about. Somehow I think the Mormon presence is the root of these problems. Not blaming you, mind you. I just think there's a connection."

"Marshal, you surely don't think that any of my brethren are responsible for these deaths and this assault?" Hostility had undeniably crept into Atkins' voice.

"No, I don't, but I do think there's somehow a connection."

"Very well. I'll conduct my business here today and we'll leave at first light. Plan on staying with us a few days. You'll be more than welcomed, Marshal."

"Thank you, Mr. Atkins. I think you should postpone your business for now, however. For your own safety. Accompany me to the hotel and get a room. Stay put for the night. I'll be around. I'll see to it that no one harms you."

"I appreciate the offer, Marshal, but I'm well prepared to fend for myself," Atkins retorted, pulling back his long black jacket and revealing a polished Colt .45.

"Good. Just be careful."

Atkins nodded in reply. "I'm sorry if I seem a bit testy. I suppose we're all becoming somewhat defensive."

"Understood. No problem." Jake could hear Caspar calming the small crowd and could see people reluctantly beginning to disperse.

"Let's go out the back way. I'll walk with you to the hotel, then see you again in the morning."

The two men caused a stir as they walked resolutely down the boardwalk. "I'm beholden, Marshal. I guess misery does love company. My fellow neighbors look none too friendly."

"Yeah. I can see that."

Morning found the two men underway by sunrise. They rode swiftly to escape observation by any early risers. After a few miles, however, by unspoken consent, they slowed to a walk. Soon Atkins began to talk, as Jake hoped he might.

"We've been settled in the canyon for some years. About the same time that Freeman was founded, really. We're a small settlement, but we've been prosperous. The Lord has been good to us."

Jake only nodded, waiting for the man to divulge information that might prove helpful. Instead, his talk turned to his faith and the controversy surrounding the practice of polygamy. Jake didn't want to hear such prattle, but he allowed the man to continue uninterrupted. He knew if he began to ask questions that Atkins might cease being cooperative and open.

"Many people object to the practice of polygamy because they do not interpret the Bible correctly. Polygamy is entirely a biblical tradition, particularly in the Old Testament. It's clear by our prosperity that this ancient Semitic custom is pleasing to our Heavenly Father."

"How many wives you got?" Jake finally asked.

"I have only four. Three are currently with child. One is, well, one is difficult. I'm hoping motherhood changes her surly manner. I fear I should never have brought her west. She should have remained at the orphanage I ordered her from. But, with time and prayer I'm certain she'll come around. I do not wish to use a heavy hand with the woman, but there's a limit to any man's patience."

Suddenly all attention, Jake found it preposterous yet entirely possible that the difficult wife could be Betsy's missing sister, Margaret. That she might be difficult came as no surprise, but the odds of her even being in the canyon seemed blatantly too coincidental. He wanted to ask more but refrained, hoping he'd be able to meet all the women that evening.

Halfway down the perilously steep descent into the canyon, Atkins pulled up. "I found her there," he said, pointing to a rocky ledge some ten feet wide and running off the trail at an angle.

"Hold my horse. I need to look around," Jake said as he dismounted. Once on the ledge the blood-spattered rocks became apparent. It was obvious she had to have fallen -- or jumped -- from the top of the steep cliff that sloped upward and outward at an angle. The mountainside here bore a sheer granite face, however. Only near the peak of the formidable gradient was there any sign of a rock formation other than slick, rock wall. No wonder she'd been so broken up. A plunge from that height would be utterly deadly.

He studied the rocky ledge but found nothing that added to his investigation. "I'll have to investigate that point tomorrow when I leave," he said to Atkins as he mounted for the final descent into the canyon.

"I've never explored the area up there, but I'm sure it's accessible," Atkins said.

Now Jake easily saw why the trip gave folks pause. He himself didn't care to make the journey again.

"You go up and down this route often?" Jake asked, trying not to look at the sheer drop-off over the narrow ledge, hoping his horse's large feet would fit on the pencil-thin trail.

Atkins laughed. "You get used to it. It definitely keeps intruders at bay. Not much company down here."

"I don't imagine."

Finally the constricted trail spilled out onto the sandy floor of the canyon. The sound of gurgling water and the singing of birds cheerily greeted the two riders as they emerged from the brush-covered trailhead. The tension in Jake's back and shoulders from the difficult descent slowly began to ease. He saw that the canyon, narrow at the entry end, widened considerably farther on. Jake rode along, enthralled by the beauty of the area, a vastly different world than the sandy, barren desert more than a thousand feet above. Towering pine, massive cottonwoods, and a variety of brush grew abundantly along the banks of the river. A few trees appeared to grow out of rock walls, their roots stubbornly clinging to fissures in the stone. Large boulders lay strewn about, but none appeared to have fallen recently as all appeared to be firmly embedded in the soft, sandy soil.

"Beautiful, isn't it?" Atkins asked, smiling for the first time, his eyes lighting up.

"Unbelievable. I've never seen anything like it."

"Then you've not been to the other canyons?"

"No. Heard about 'em. Haven't been there yet."

"Ah! It's glorious splendor such as you'll never see elsewhere on the face of the earth, of that I can assure you."

"How many people live down here?" Jake asked.

"Upwards of two hundred eighty-five."

"There's plenty of space?"

"Dear sir, you're seeing only a small portion here. In some areas the floor of the canyon is two or more miles wide. This particular canyon is more than twenty miles in length, although it twists and curves a great deal at the westerly end. Other canyons intersect here, also. Each feature the same amenities as this one. We call this canyon Bishop's Bastion. All are teeming with life, good soil, water, and timber. We have everything that we need, and more. It's truly our own little Eden. Paradise on Earth."

"So, you go into Freeman for...?"

"Trade for the few supplies we cannot raise here ourselves. Things like sugar, for example. A luxury for certain, but a lovely one. We sell our surplus goods there. Often deliver barrels of water."

"That must be interesting – getting the water up there."

"Oh, we have excellent mules for that. Sure-footed, strong little beasts, I assure you. There's another trail out, of course, that we use for pack trains. It emerges much farther from Freeman, however. At one time we talked of building a pipeline of sorts so the water could be pumped, but many in the group did not wish to support this effort, mostly because no one was even sure it could be done. It would be an extraordinary engineering feat, certainly."

Was water the issue behind the crimes? Maybe it was the land itself. There was no comparison between dusty, gritty little Freeman and the lush, beautiful vista he now saw unfolding. The air, humid from the heat and running water, carried fragrances Jake had seldom before smelled.

An hour later, after crossing the meandering river many times, Jake saw chimney smoke ahead. One more bend, then before him, set in a dense cluster of tall pine trees, lay a picturesque village consisting of a dozen or more moderately sized, sturdily constructed log and wood buildings. Shaded, dirt pathways seemed to connect all the edifices.

"This is our community center, you might say. About thirty people live here full time. The rest live down river. Some farm; others raise cattle, chickens, all the usual animals one would find on any farm or ranch."

"I'm impressed, Mr. Atkins. I must say this is hard to believe. It's so...." Jake searched for the right words, but realized only the word "quiet" immediately came to mind. "Where is everyone?"

"The women, most naturally, are indoors tending to their chores. The few men who live here in the center still farm and tend to their animals, only returning at dusk. Please, come this way. My stable boy will take care of your horse. Have no worries," he added quickly when Jake hesitated. "I assure you, everything in this valley is safe."

A young Navajo boy came forth to take the mounts. "This is James. He and his family are newly converted to our faith," Atkins volunteered. "We have many Indian converts here in the canyon," he added. Then, "Take good care of Marshal Silver's fine horse, James."

Jake smiled and reluctantly surrendered his mount to the boy's care. Turning to the house he suddenly stopped, momentarily speechless. The girl stood there, the sun seeming to caress her upturned face. It clearly was not Betsy, but so alike did the two sisters look that there was no doubt it had to be Margaret, and an expectant Margaret at that. She stood taller and heavier than Betsy, with light brown hair instead of blonde, but there was no mistaking the facial features. Even from where he stood, Jake could see the large, piercing, sky-blue eyes, the delicate upturned nose, and perfect oval face.

"Margaret, dear, we have a guest this evening. Please remember the things we've talked about."

The girl glared at Jeremiah Atkins, and Jake instantly knew, but was not in the least surprised, that she was the difficult one, the orphan from New York that Atkins had spoken of.

Surreptitiously he watched the girl sullenly turn toward the entry, hesitate in the doorway as she turned again to watch the two men, then slowly turn back and disappear into the darkened house.

"She should not be seen in her present condition. I hope you'll excuse her brazenness," Atkins half-apologized. "She has simply not accepted our way of life, despite our best efforts. I have yet to lay a hand on her, but I am truly at my wit's end. No woman should be so stubborn. She is most definitely the rogue, if you get my meaning."

"Yes, I have a good idea what you're talking about," Jake answered, thinking of Betsy and her stubborn determination.

"I'll show you to your room where you may wash up and rest if you wish. Dinner is served at 5:00 every evening. Feel free to join us for worship later, if you please. Of course you are welcome and completely free to look around our community and make yourself at home."

"Thank you, I'll just do that."

Despite his fatigue, Jake was interested in seeing a Mormon community first hand. Mostly impressed, he nevertheless took umbrage with the seeming indenture of Margaret DuBonnet. How many other women lived here not of their own free will? he wondered. Should he try to speak with Margaret privately? Tell her of Betsy? Her condition made it obvious that he would not be able to take her from the canyon on this trip. He wasn't familiar with women in her state, but judging by her bulging middle he guessed she was pretty far along with child. It would be some time before she'd be able to leave. The legality of it all eluded him, also. He'd need to make certain of the law before he acted. Was he even in Arizona now, or was this Utah? Did it matter? But at least he could tell Betsy where Margaret was and that she was safe. Should he tell her? What if Betsy took off on her own to rescue her sister?

One of the wives served dinner promptly at 5:00 p.m., but Jake was disappointed when the two men dined alone. Atkins assured him that the women simply preferred not to be around strangers, particularly in their delicate conditions, he added. After dinner Atkins retired along with other members of the group to a large building used for worship services, while Jake took an extended stroll around the compound.

The setting, the grounds, the dwellings all seemed just about as perfect as one could wish. This indeed appeared to be a harmonious environment, save for the reclusiveness and isolation of the community. Despite all appearances otherwise, Jake sensed that somehow these people were not truly free, but rather ruled by an invisible, iron-fisted tyrant. Things were too orderly. Too quiet. Where were all the children? He heard no chatter, no laughter. The canyon seemed more of a prison to him now. But what did he know? Perhaps people sought this solace and solitude for good reason. He strolled about for an hour, stopping by the barn to check on his horse. The young Navajo boy met him at the doorway and smiled, then led him to the stall where Jake's steed stood, contentedly munching fresh, sweet alfalfa.

"We got a big climb tomorrow, Buddy. You best eat and drink while you can," he said softly to the large animal. The horse would most certainly be wired with energy after its sumptuous dinner.

Leaving the barn, he wandered to the river. Here the icy cold water flowed quickly, and he saw that the current ran even more swiftly in the deeper sections. Standing at the water's edge, he again surveyed the settlement. Everywhere he saw flower boxes and small gardens. Water here was obviously not in short supply. Intuitively he knew that somehow this settlement, this area, was the root cause of the murders and kidnappings, but he could only sense the connection. He had no evidence whatsoever to prove his hunch. The area was closed to non-Mormon investors and settlers. Did these people have something that others wanted so badly they'd kill for it? He'd seen it happen before. Ranchers killed so widows would sell out. How many times had he seen a man murdered so that another could woo and wed the deceased's wife or sweetheart? He'd have to talk with Eliot, the land speculator. The man oozed oily charm, but kept lousy company. Jake knew for certain that Fernley had done time for robbery and murder. The culprit exuded bad news.

Jake'd leave in the morning. No one here would be able to tell him anything about the murders or the kidnappings. He'd investigate the area at the top of Diablo Peak. Maybe there he'd find evidence pertaining to the dead girl. He finally returned to the quiet house, disappointed he hadn't seen or spoken to Margaret. He momentarily thought of Betsy but brusquely brushed her from his mind.

Return

OVER the next weeks, the storms became intermittent, but Betsy lingered. Shaun physically improved on a daily basis, but still she forestalled her departure. During their time together, he taught her to wet mine, and she helped him with his gold mining. He told her he loved to hear her shriek with happy laughter when tiny gold flakes remained in her pan. Her merry voice, he said, sounded like Marie's, and it warmed his heart.

Her cooking improved dramatically, and with practice her shooting skills became superb. Every day that she left with the rifle, she returned with small game, and Shaun taught her to skin and gut the catch, pointing out which organs were edible and which best avoided. He also taught her how to use the juice from the ocotillo limbs as a poultice, which he applied to his leg when it swelled and pained him. He showed her the strange, long-stemmed plants which he brewed into Mormon Tea. The two picked the fruit from the mesquite, ground it into a meal, added water, and made it into flat, edible cakes. "Just like my mud pies," she said, laughing.

He told her he wanted to prepare her, knowing she would be leaving soon, and he wanted to give her the basic skills she'd need to survive.

One day he announced they would be taking a trip to Sally's Station, a good day's ride away.

"I need to check on one of my mine claims. I've got a partner there – one I don't entirely trust."

"How many claims do you have?"

"A few, that's certain. I've got half a dozen in the Stanton area. One's up past Sally's Station, and a few are spread out in the desert between Wickenburg and Stanton. I like this one here in the summer because of the water. It's cooler working on the river than in the kiln-hot, bloody desert out there."

They left early, riding a few miles down the Hassayampa before Shaun angled his mule onto a sandy path hidden by bushes. Mid morning found them on a hard-packed, uphill trail that switch-backed up the mountainside. It was rough going, and as they left the cooler air by the river, the temperature quickly became unbearably hot. The spectacular view kept Betsy from complaining, however, and every time she looked behind, the river valley's serenity and rugged beauty astonished her. It was so different from New York City and from her plantation home in Georgia. This was another world entirely.

"Quite a sight, isn't it?" Shaun asked, watching her.

"It's so magnificent! Why would people live in ugly cities when they could live here and see this beautiful scenery every day?"

"Well, beauty's in the eye of the beholder, they say. Every place has its advantages – and disadvantages as well."

"What could be so bad about living here?"

"Men pretty much get away with murder here, Betsy. You know that first hand. Doctors are few.

It's not a place for a woman, that's certain. This life destroys women, most of them anyway."

"Well, I love it. I've always dreamed of living somewhere that's very isolated. I want a cabin and flowers."

He smiled warmly at her dreams. "Keep your dreams, girl. Sometimes they've a way of comin' true. I'm dreamin' of takin' a break here soon. We'll stop in a bit and give the horses a rest. This here's a long, hot climb."

They entered the scorching wash in the afternoon, and a short distance later they came to the Station. Nestled in a profusion of green trees and shrubbery, the station building and lush surroundings reminded Betsy of the oases she'd read about.

She contented herself with sitting in the shade while Shaun went about his business. He introduced her as Marie's daughter, and the few folk present doted on her, having met Marie on one of Shaun's former trips.

The station seemed busy compared to the quiet and isolation of the claim along the Hassayampa.

Miners came and went, wagons arrived, much shouting and raucous laughter issued from the buildings. She observed it all, another world. Shaun was right. Despite its beauty, this world was deadly.

The return trip the following day, almost all downhill, went significantly faster than had the long pull uphill, and Betsy was relieved to be back in the surroundings along the Hassayampa that had become so familiar to her.

With the return, however, without a word being said, they both understood that she would leave soon. Her time with him had come to an end. He loved her as a daughter, but she was not his daughter, and he knew that she was enough like her mother that she would do as she willed, no matter how he might plead, argue, cajole, or condemn her decision.

By all accounts it was now July. Thunder clouds often piled on the far mountain rims and put on dazzling displays of activity in the distance, but it had been weeks since it'd rained in their area. Betsy grew more and more restless, withdrawing into herself. She hoped he understood, on a visceral level, that no matter what he said, she wouldn't stay, and it pained her to have to hurt him like this.

"Living with an old bachelor up the Hassyampa River is not a place for a beautiful, young girl," he said one night after supper. "I know it's time for ya to leave, Betsy, though I sorely lament seeing ya go."

She nodded, indicating that she fully understood what he said.

"I can take you to Prescott. It'd be my pleasure. I'm owin' ya, lass. You saved my life. I know nothin' I do can ever repay you, but I want you to know I'd lay down my life for ya."

"Thank you, Shaun. I think that's the most noble thing anyone's ever said to me," she said, a sad smile visiting her face. "But you don't owe me anything. Just knowing you took good care of my mama, and that you loved her so much, is all that matters to me. I'll never forget that, or you, either."

"Well, if you're set on goin' I want you to have a few things," he said, turning and disappearing into the tent. When he returned he held his prized weapon. "Take this rifle and scabbard." He affixed the Henry in its case to her saddle. "You're a good shot now, girl, and I'm proud of ya. And I want you to take that blanket what was your mama's, and take this too," he added, handing her two small leather pouches filled with gold coins. "There's a couple hundred dollars there. It's not doin' me any good sittin' here in this tent. I got no need for it. I got plenty more. Plenty more. Besides, you earned it pannin' for all that gold dust."

"Shaun, I…"

"No thanks needed, lass. You just be careful," he said with affection as she hugged him. "Guess I better be callin' you Tom Black now."

***

Neither slept well that night. Shaun lay awake wondering what would happen to the girl on the cot across from him. He tried to picture only happy scenarios, but inevitably a black scene would dash his dreams for her. Indians might be troublesome, especially for a person traveling alone. He doubted her disguise would fool an Indian for very long, but ruffians and outlaws were his main concern. She was a delicate flower that he cringed to think of some hooligan destroying. She rode well. She shot well. She even cooked well. But she was much too lovely for her own good.

He consoled himself with the thought that she had gotten this far without incurring any real harm. Perhaps she had a heavenly protector lookin' out for her. It amazed him, when he thought on it, how far she'd come unscathed. She'd certainly fared better than her mother had.

Marie had confessed her troubled past to him the first night he'd brought her up river. She'd told him of her illegal indenture to the bankrupt, ruined plantation owner who'd quickly turned his attention to her, a young, helpless French girl, as a substitute for his sickly wife. Marie bore two daughters as a result of the nocturnal visits by the master of the house. He kept her bound to him by threatening to sell her little babes. Not until the man turned his evil eye toward Margaret did Marie steal away in the night with her children. He'd sold Marie many times to his friends to help keep the ramshackle remnants of his plantation standing, but she would not allow him to ruin her daughters.

She'd taken the girls to New York in hopes of obtaining factory work, but her efforts had been an abysmal failure. Despite finding employment, she'd been unable to support the three of them. Ultimately, she'd begged for help at the orphanage, and they'd lived there for two years before she volunteered to be transported west. She could not fault the orphanage burdened with just too many mouths to feed. She agreed to marry a man, a stranger, but it turned out that he was killed the day before her arrival. John Casey stepped in after she sat on a bench for over a day, with no money and nowhere to go. Men had strutted by continually, looking her over as though she were chattel. Whistling and lewdly winking, some even sat beside her and wrapped their arms about her until she pushed them away. John Casey saved her. But John Casey had a mean streak, especially when he drank, and Marie had been the victim of his violent, vicious outbursts on more than one occasion.

Shaun rolled to his side. Thoughts of Marie made him weep. And now he had to stand by and watch Betsy go off into an unfriendly, unforgiving wilderness filled with crooks, criminals, and murderers.

The next morning, to keep her from the nosy, unruly Wickenburg inhabitants, he accompanied her to a wash that would lead her to Stanton. "Once in Stanton, stay on the stagecoach road, Betsy. You've got money enough now, so I don't want you campin' out any longer. If you weren't so attached to that fine animal you're ridin', I'd insist you take the coach." He drew her a rough map, showing the outline of the mountains behind Stanton. "If'n you leave the wash because of the rains, just head for these peaks. They'll be visible from most anywhere out on the flats."

"Thank you, Shaun. Thank you for everything," she said with a shaky voice. "You've been like a father to me these past few weeks. I've never had a father, and I'd proudly claim you. I'll come back to see you someday, I promise!" She bit her lower lip, but he saw it quiver.

"Go on, now. You get going so you can make it to Stanton before dark."

As he watched, she headed Moonlight down the wash, turning once to wave goodbye. "You be careful, Tom Black," he called after her as tears filled his eyes. "You be careful."

He would go to Wickenburg now. He had business that must not wait.

Arrest

DESPITE Jeremiah Atkins' repeated efforts to entice him to spend another day, Jake left early for the difficult trek up the side of the canyon walls. Atkins drew a map pointing out good resting places, assuring Jake the steepest part was the first half mile of the trail. The remainder would be steep, but manageable by an animal--or human--in good condition. Atkins rode with Jake as far as the semi-hidden entrance, then bid him adieu, wishing him Godspeed.

During the murderous ascent, Jake's horse kept a slow, steady pace. Even though the horse was not yet winded, Jake chose to stop at the first open flat spot he came to, and to take a full fifteen-minute break before remounting. Forty-five minutes into the ascent he passed the area where Atkins had found Susie Gatch's broken, battered body. He stopped and dismounted, thinking perhaps he'd missed something yesterday. Studying the cliff face, he blinked rapidly. Had he seen a glint? He saw the smoke before he heard the shot, but he instinctively took refuge behind a large rock. Peering around the boulder, he now saw definite movement at the top of Diablo Peak. Two, maybe three people scurried about. No one seemed too interested in him yet. Making a quick decision, he grabbed his horse's reins and headed up the trail on foot. Fifty feet farther up, the narrow trail bent around a bluff, which would keep him out of sight of the shooters for a bit. The way was steep, and despite the adrenaline coursing through his body, he doubted he could continue to scramble up the side of the mountain at this pace. He wasn't out of breath, but he stopped anyway to give his pounding heart a chance to settle before he made the next dash for safety. He'd be exposed on the next bend of the trail, but worse, he'd be unable to fire a shot off, even though he'd be easy pickings for anyone above choosing to shoot at him. He hesitated briefly, then scampered up the steep mountainside, hoping to be at least partially protected by the large protruding rocks. Slapping his horse soundly on the rear, he prayed the animal would continue safely up the trail. "If you bastards kill my horse I'll kill you with my bare hands," he muttered through clenched teeth.

They were now taking only potshots at him, obviously waiting for him to move into the open. Bullets struck rocks around him, sending shards in all directions and small rocks cascading down the almost perpendicular cliff.

Suddenly, Jake remembered he'd left his rifle with the horse. "Damn it to hell." A costly error, he'd now have to move within handgun range in order to shoot back. What had he been thinking? It wasn't like him to make this kind of blunder. He paused, dismayed at his oversight. He needed his rifle. The Colt was good, but it wasn't the same as his rifle, that's all there was to it. He tried to comfort himself with the thought that whoever was shooting at him didn't know that he didn't have a rifle, so they wouldn't expect him to close in on them. Overconfident, they might let down their guard. Perhaps he could work this impossible situation to his advantage.

Still angry, he knew he had to settle down to avoid any more costly mistakes. He continued his climb, trying to study the terrain at the top of the hill. He soon realized he had no choice. He'd have to leave the safety of the boulders and cross the trail to the right. They wouldn't be expecting that. They'd be watching for him to appear below their lair. He'd approach them from an unexpected angle. Would it, he wondered, be possible to make it to the top and circle around behind them? On foot it could possibly be a two-hour climb, but doable. He had to keep out of their line of sight for as long as possible. If he managed to cross to the other side of the trail without being seen, he'd make it. They wouldn't be looking for him to do that. He only hoped that he'd find places to access the trail once in a while without being seen.

Slowly and steadily, as the full force of the sun shone on the mountain face, Jake continued his climb. He had no water because he'd also left his canteen on the horse. Sweat drenched, he rested twice in the ascent, even though he didn't feel the need to stop. He knew he was dehydrated and would not be at his peak performance. He reasoned that the rest would help him sustain some energy.

He'd climbed more quickly than he thought he could, until only a couple of hundred feet remained between him and the top of the canyon wall. He swung wider, not wanting to chance that they might see or hear him. Occasional shots glanced off rocks far away from where he now climbed. So far his plan was working. The shooters still thought he was ascending the face from directly below them. Voices taunted and jeered. Laughter and a few rifle shots followed each outburst. Amusing themselves, they weren't paying attention. Jake surmised that the malefactors weren't terribly bright.

He paused before emerging onto the barren mesa at the top of the canyon. His horse stood not five feet away grazing on wild bunch grass. Jake smiled, pulled himself onto the flat ground, took the horse's reins, and secured him to a large sagebrush. The sage would never hold if the horse panicked and ran, but it would at least keep the animal from following him to the rock formation that housed his would-be assassins several hundred yards away. He grabbed his rifle, then drank some water, happy that the playing field had just been leveled. He was good with a gun, real good, but not great. He was, however, great with a rifle. He'd never been outshot and had been blessed with tremendous distance vision.

Having no cover now, Jake bent and ran swiftly and silently, loaded rifle in hand, hoping to get to the rocky configuration without being seen. Then, and only then, would the element of surprise be his.

Breathing slowly and quietly, he lay back against the sharp, hot rock and checked his revolver. Not knowing which direction around the mound to proceed, he decided to climb to the top of the outcropping. If he could maintain absolute silence in the climb, he'd arrive undetected and completely safe from return fire.

Suddenly, he heard voices approaching from a path on the left side of the outcropping. He spun to the right and squatted behind the shelter of the solid knoll.

"I don't see how he coulda got by us, Johnny. I was watchin' the whole damn time. I'm tellin' ya, I think he headed back down."

"We're not paid to think, Reub. Frank'll have a fit when he finds out we let that sumbitch get away."

"Stop right there and drop your weapons," Jake shouted from his concealed position.

Both men halted, but neither lowered their rifles.

"I said drop your guns. You're under arrest for the murder of Suzanna Gatch," Jake yelled.

Slowly the two men turned. A wry smile crossed Johnny's face. Jake recognized him immediately as Johnny "Quick Draw" Geiger. He didn't know the companion.

"Well, my good friend, Jake Silver," Geiger drawled. "Heard you got yourself a new job and big promotion. Got tired of punching cows, huh?"

Geiger drawled. "Long time since Fort Worth. How's that sister of yours, by the way? She still beggin' for me to stop by every night?"

"Good to see you too, Johnny. Now shut your mouth and throw down your weapons. Don't get any stupid ideas."

Johnny Geiger, a dashing, good-looking young man, had a way of needling a man until he grew crazed enough to draw on him. Geiger had gotten away with numerous murders because witnesses always testified that the victim drew first. This was true, but no one ever mentioned that Geiger could push any sane man over the edge of sanity just by his sneer and obscene references to a man's wife or sweetheart. His handsome looks belied a cold, cunning, murderous nature. He beat his women, picked on cripples, and stirred up trouble wherever he went.

"Well now, Marshal. We got us a small problem here. See, we don't wanna throw down. We ain't done nothin' illegal 'cept maybe engage in a little target practice. Is that what you so uppity about? We don't know any Suzanna Gatch, do we, Reuben?"

Jake heard small rocks crunch behind him. He turned and fired blindly, then turned back in time to feel the sting of Geiger's bullet in his right bicep before he could thumb the trigger again. Geiger took off running, but Reuben Walsh made the mistake of drawing down. It was his last gunfight.

Rolling quickly, Jake raised his weapon to fire behind him again, but saw only a half-clad girl, pale as death itself, her eyes vacant, now standing beside the rock, apparently not caring if she lived or died.

He swiftly arose, pushing the girl down behind the safety of the boulder. Looking into her lifeless eyes, he stopped himself from asking if she was okay. "Stay here. I'll be back. You're safe now." Unresponsive, she laid her head against the rock, staring dumbly at nothing.

Ignoring the injury to his arm, Jake took careful aim and fired at the fleeing Geiger. He hated shooting a man in the back, but perhaps he'd make an exception for Geiger. Aiming for a leg, hoping to cripple the fleeing outlaw, his shot flew high, hitting Johnny in the side. Johnny grabbed his side, but he kept moving until he disappeared into a grove of mesquite where the two outlaws kept their horses tethered. Raising his rifle, Jake stepped from his cover to take another shot. Finding Geiger obscured by the heavy growth, he spent his ebbing energy in pursuit, dismayed when the culprit made a clean escape on horseback.

A litany of profanity spilled from him. Stunned at his bad shot, he returned to the lifeless Reuben Walsh, muttering a long string of swear words as he made certain that the outlaw was indeed dead. Ripping off Walsh's shirt, he turned his attention to the nearly comatose girl, wrapping it about the girl's shoulders.

"What's your name?" Jake asked gently.

When the girl didn't answer, he tried again. "My name is Marshal Silver. I'm here to help you. What's your name?"

After a moment, she turned her stony eyes upon him. "Patsy Baker," she whispered. "Please don't tell anyone! Don't tell anyone about…this…."

"Patsy, where's the other girl?"

"Suzanna jumped. Victoria's in the cave. When we tried to get away, they tied us up. They said they were going to kill us today." Her monotone voice faded to a whisper and she began mumbling to herself.

"Patsy, stay here. I'm going to get Victoria. I'll be right back."

"Victoria's dead. Killed herself."

Jake shook his head sadly. He needed to kill Geiger. Even if he had to spend the rest of his career hunting the man down, he'd shoot the bastard, pure and simple. He'd kill Frank Fernley, too.

He stood, surveying the scene. The race up the mountainside had left him spent, but he needed to muster the energy to tie Walsh and the dead Victoria to one horse and take Patsy with him on his.

His arm began to throb now that the crisis had passed. He'd have to get moving soon before he lost his ability to move the limb. The wound would need to be tended to before he developed an infection and lost an arm. After a quick check, he surmised that the injury looked worse than it actually was. The bullet had deeply grazed his arm, causing it to bleed profusely. It would probably self-clean, but he'd see a doctor as soon as possible anyway. He didn't imagine a one-armed marshal would be very effective.

Retrieving his horse and finding Walsh's mount in the thicket of mesquite, he set about the gruesome task of securing dead, and half-dead, bodies. He hoped that Geiger would still be around by the time he got down to hunting him. He doubted it, but a man's pride sometimes got the best of him.

Despite his urgency to return to Freeman and start his manhunt, he spent half an hour snooping through the men's lair in the cave. Outside the entry he found a number of .50 caliber shell casings. Neither Geiger nor Walsh had carried a

Sharps. The casings had to have come from Fernley's rifle, the one Jake had seen outside Bell's office. Not many men carried a Sharps unless they hunted buffalo, which Fernley did not. Jake had no doubt now that Fernley made up the third member of the dastardly trio.

Arriving in Freeman late, Jake rousted Sheriff Caspar who summoned Doc Helman, who also served as the undertaker. "Well, I'll have some business for awhile," the doctor said, looking over the two individuals tied to the horse outside Caspar's office and the two sitting in inside, waiting for medical care.

While the doc tended to Jake's wound, Jake gave a statement to Caspar. "I think you may want to question Bell and Eliot," he said. "I'd like to be present, if you don't mind."

"Not at all," Caspar readily agreed. "I'm gettin' too old for this kind of trouble. Didn't realize it until I seen the condition of these young girls..." he paused, uncertain how to describe the tortured, terrorized girls. "Just gettin' too old for this. Times has changed. Time was women and children were off limits. This new breed of desperados would savage their own mothers."

Jake only nodded.

"I've made up my mind to retire when this fiasco's over. The town's dyin' anyway. The law needs new blood. Young men like yourself who got more nerves than good sense. You know what I mean," he added apologetically.

"I think Eliot and Bell have been trying to run the Mormons out so they can take over the land in the canyons. You been down there, Charles?"

The old sheriff shook his head.

"It's incredible. I've never seen anything like it. I can see why a man might covet such property. I think they'd schemed to get folks to blame the Mormons, but folks only thought of the Indians. I haven't figured out the actual plan yet, but I got a feeling Eliot and Bell are in on it, whatever it is. Frank Fernley's bad news, and he's fully one with them, along with Geiger and Walsh, who were probably just hired to do the dirty work."

"I'll get Bell over here first thing in the morning. He'll talk quicker than Eliot will. Bein' an attorney and all, though, he'll know his rights."

"Make it more like ten. That'll give him time to get good and nervous. Maybe he'll make a foolish move. I'll be here by ten. I want to talk to the banker and see what I can find out on Eliot. Meanwhile, keep an eye out for Geiger. He's wounded and may seek help."

Well after midnight, Jake collapsed onto his lumpy bed. He hoped Geiger or Fernley didn't show up because he knew he'd never hear them coming.

***

They say bad news travels fast, and judging by the empty streets of Freeman the next morning, Jake had no doubt that the town knew there was bad business afloat. He ate a big breakfast, having had no lunch or dinner the day before. Sheriff Caspar showed up just as he was finishing.

"Just coffee," the sheriff said, nodding to the cranky, harried waitress. Then to Jake he said, "I been thinking about our talk last night, Marshal. I think we need to arrest those two culprits before they sneak on outta town."

Jake agreed. "Tell you what. I'll head on over to Bell's office now. He's lowered his shade since I came in the restaurant. You arrest Eliot. I'll bring Bell in. I think I can get him to spill his guts easy enough. Let's just walk on out of here nice and easy like we don't have a care in the world. Keep them off guard if they're watching."

Both men left the café and headed in different directions. Jake began a stroll down the boardwalk, pausing often to look into store fronts, but in actuality using the glass to mirror Bell's office to ascertain if he was being watched. Close to the end of the long street where no one could see him from the angle of the law office, he casually crossed the road and entered an alley. Now, completely out of sight, he broke into a run, emerged from the passageway, and turned sharply left, skirting the backsides of the buildings, quickly making his way to the back of Bell's office.

Pausing outside the back entry, Jake pulled his Colt from its holster and checked the loaded chamber. Undecided whether to kick in the door or quietly slip in and catch the occupants off guard, he hesitated. Three or four people might be in the small office, which would make it almost impossible to enter unnoticed. Bell, Eliot, Fernley, and maybe even Geiger could be present. Fernley and Geiger would most likely be armed, so he'd go for them first. Both men were deadly and had nothing to lose. Maybe he should shoot first and worry about legalities later.

Taking a deep breath, he reared back and kicked the door handle squarely with all of his two hundred pounds, the loud splintering announcing the arrival of trouble.

The element of surprise caught all three men off guard. Colt cocked, Jake leaped through the door, spinning toward Fernley. Slowly rising, Fernley dropped his hand toward his gun.

"Hold it right there, Fernley," Jake shouted. "Don't do something stupid and get yourself killed." Turning his attention to Bell's ashen face and Eliot's livid looks, he ordered both men to rise slowly and put their hands atop their heads. In a flash he saw Fernley go for his gun, which he'd fully expected. The deafening roar of the Colt in the enclosed quarters silenced the sound of Fernley crumpling backwards and breaking the chair to splinters as he crashed to the floor.

Before Fernley hit the ground, Jake spun, riveting his attention to the two remaining men, his eyes catching their every twitch.

"Don't move, gentlemen. I shoot to kill and will be glad to do so. Just give me a reason and you're dead like your friend here."

"Don't shoot," Clifford Bell wailed. "I'll tell you everything you want to know. It wasn't my idea. None of this was."

"Shut up, Bell. If you know what's good for you, you'll shut that flappin' trap right now or...." Eliot stopped, seeming to suddenly remember the position he was in.

"Or what, Eliot? Stay away from that drawer, Bell!" Jake snapped as Bell inched his hand toward the small desk drawer. "I don't care whether I shoot you or hang you. Either way's the same to me."

Neither man spoke, but their faces distorted with myriad emotions. "Let's go, boys. I'm sure the sheriff has some accommodations for you."

"What will happen to me?" Bell asked, his eyes bulging in fear.

"Looks like you'll be taking a little trip to Prescott to stand trial, Mr. Bell."

"But I've committed no crime!"

"That'll be up to a jury to decide. Now quit your blabbin' and turn around. Keep your hands on your head. You too, Eliot."

Both men complied as ordered, Bell responding obediently, Eliot reluctantly. Jake removed Eliot's pistol and quickly patted the man down, retrieving a knife also. Bell was clean. After securing both men's wrists, he said, "Let's go. Walk slow. If you make a run for it, you're dead. It'd give me great pleasure to finish you off after what happened to those little girls."

"I had nothing to do with that," Bell protested vehemently. "I swear to you. I'm innocent. I told Eliot to make Fernley stop his barbarism."

"Shut up, you sniveling rat," Eliot hissed. "He's got nothin' on us. Look, Marshal, it was Fernley and his boys through and through. We never touched those girls. Never had nothing to do with nothing."

"Eliot, save it for someone who cares. Start walking before I shoot you out of boredom."

Shortly the men stood behind bars.

"Fernley's dead," Jake informed Caspar. "You better have someone retrieve his body."

"The judge won't be passing through here for another six months, if then, Marshal. What should I do with them until then?"

"I'm taking them back to Prescott with me to stand trial."

Obviously relieved, Caspar asked, "What can I do to help?"

"I could use a wagon. It'll be safer transporting these two if they're not riding. I'll see to it that the wagon gets returned."

"Consider it done. When will you be leaving?"

"In a few days. Meanwhile, see if you can get Bell to talk. He's ready. Keep Eliot locked up, but I think Bell can be safely removed from the cell if you keep him shackled. He'll talk if he's not around Eliot."

"What'll you be doing?"

"I'm going on a hunt for Johnny Geiger. When I find him I'll be back to fetch these two."

"Don't delay, Marshal. This is more commotion than this old man can stand. I'm mighty uncomfortable with these goings-on."

Jake smiled and patted the stooping sheriff's back. "You're doing great, Chalres. I mean that. Rest assured, I'll be back soon."

Ambush

BETSY headed up the wash as directed. Shaun had drawn a detailed map of every turn, plus an excellent sketch of the mountains rising behind Stanton. "If nothing else," he'd told her, "just ride toward this area," and he'd circled a flat mountain. "Stanton will be sittin' there pretty as you please. With the gold they're haulin' outta there, no one's goin' nowhere."

It didn't look all that far, and Agar had assured her it wasn't. "Once you're in Stanton, it's an uphill ride to Yarnell. From there you can be in Prescott in two days if you keep movin'. You've got money, lass. You stay in hotels. No camping. Stay on the stagecoach road, Betsy. You promise me?"

She'd nodded, but Shaun would not accept a mere nod.

"No, lass. Let me hear you say it."

"Okay," Betsy laughed. "Shaun, I promise I won't camp along the way. I promise I'll stay in a hotel."

After turning around once to wave goodbye, she urged Moonlight into a trot since it seemed to be easier for the horse to move through the sand at a trot than a walk. But she had to be careful not to run him too much, for she knew it would soon grow to be intolerably hot, and with no breeze, she didn't know if she could even continue this route. Shaun had told her to stay off the roads lest she be robbed or worse by vagabonds and other travelers, but the road soon seemed the lesser of two evils.

Sweat quickly drenched her, and even though she carried an extra canteen, she felt she'd best ration the water. She also had to keep an eye on the weather. She'd learned over the past few weeks that even if it wasn't raining in her area, a storm ten miles or more away could result in a torrential flooding, mud and debris roaring unexpectedly down a dry wash far from the storm.

She would stay the night in Stanton and, at Shaun's request, she'd stay in the hotel. After that it would be two days, maybe three, to Prescott.

She was only returning to Prescott because she had nowhere else to go. At least there she knew Miss Hall, whom she, Miss Elizabeth DuBonnet, personally could now pay for her room and board and Moonlight's keep because of Shaun's generosity. She remembered a few other individuals who'd been welcoming and kind to her.

But she most definitely did not want to cross paths with Jake Silver ever, ever again. She didn't think that would be a problem based on his ignoring her, but she found herself cringing anyway when she imagined what would transpire if she were to run into him somewhere. He hadn't come by to say goodbye before he'd left town like he promised, either. By her reckoning, she'd been gone now over a month, maybe six weeks, and since he hadn't showed up, she supposed he'd not even tried to find her. Anger and embarrassment needled her.

She rode on, her cheeks flaming in fury when she pictured him laughing and cavorting with other women who had status, good families and… and, oh who cared anyway? She never wanted to lay eyes on Jake Silver again.

She arrived in Stanton much earlier than expected, and barely resisted the temptation to continue, but remembering the steep climb and the brutal heat, she knew it would be better to wait until early morning before resuming the journey. It was now furnace hot and sticky, with towering white clouds gathering on the rim. She didn't at all like the idea of being caught in a fierce mountain thunderstorm, and wondered if it were possible for rain to wash out the road. She hoped not. She hesitated to admit it, even to herself, but she desperately wanted to return to Prescott.

"I'd like a room for the night," she said in her Tom Black voice to the surly, perspiring man behind the counter.

"That'll be a dollar. Sign here," he responded gruffly, turning the register toward her.

Opening one of the small leather pouches, she withdrew an eagle, knowing its value was ten dollars.

"You got anything smaller?" The clerk asked, taking the newly minted coin and turning it over and over in his hand. His scrutinizing glare nearly melted her. Did he buy her disguise?

Shaking her head no, she signed the register, then pulled her hat lower in an attempt to cover more of her face and the blonde hair now grown long enough to be gathered at the nape of her neck.

The clerk muttered and complained continually while he slowly counted out the change, blatant in his scrutiny of her.

"Where you headin'?" he asked in fake nonchalance.

"Prescott." Betsy muttered, uncertain how to avoid answering, then immediately wishing she'd said Wickenburg or some other town in the opposite direction.

"You travelin' alone?"

Wary, she stiffened slightly, but not knowing how to tell the nosy clerk to mind his own business answered simply, "Nope."

"Upstairs. Third door on the right. No baths. Café closes at eight. Bar's open 'til midnight. Poker starts at nine if you're a gamblin' man. You a gamblin' man, sonny?"

Shaking her head in reply, she walked away quickly and climbed the stairs, wishing more than ever she'd camped.

***

The clerk waited a few minutes then motioned to a heavily muscled, black-bearded man who sidled up to the counter. Resting massive, hairy forearms on the desk, he scowled at the clerk.

"That one's loaded, Mr. Hanson," the desk clerk said conspiratorially, nodding his head toward the stairs.

"How do ya know?"

"Saw it. He's got a leather pouch full of eagles and double eagles. Gotta be two, three hundred dollars at least."

"What's his name?"

The clerk swung the register toward him. "Signed in as Tom Black. Looks like a kid to me."

"Well, then, this is my lucky day. It'll be like takin' candy from a baby," Hanson sniggered.

"Don't do it here. He paid for only one night and he's travelin' alone. Headin' up the stagecoach road tomorrow. Goin' to Prescott. Easy pickin's anywhere along there."

Dan Hanson nodded in response, expertly rolling a toothpick around his mouth. After flipping a dollar onto a café table in an adjoining room, he sauntered over to the only saloon in town, seeking Curly Jones, already half drunk and deep in an argument, pounding heavily on a table in an effort to make his point.

"Got us a good one. You gonna be up for it?" Hanson asked.

"Hell, yes," Curly squinted through watering, bloodshot eyes.

"Shouldn't be too hard. Lone rider. Got a couple hundred on him in eagles. Leavin' tomorrow for Prescott."

"Think he's a good shot, or what?"

"Don't think so. Dave says he looks like a kid."

Curly cackled, rubbing his hands in glee. "That suits me jes fine. I need easy pickin's after that sonuvabitch up the Hassayampa shot me up." Still cackling, he called for a bottle of whiskey. "Put it on my tab. Pay ya tomorrow," he said to the bartender. "Need to celebrate tonight!" he sang out, raising a shot glass to his partner.

"Don't go gettin' yourself all drunked up. You know what happened last time," Hanson chided. "You're gonna limp the rest of your life because you didn't take that limey serious enough."

"Well, serves him right that the damn bitch got shot. Bastard shot me in the leg and you're right, I ain't gonna walk without a limp again."

***

Betsy sat in the growing dark of the hotel room, listening to the sounds of unruly miners and ruffians mingling on the street below. She could hear the distant rumble of thunder. She didn't want to leave the room, but she hadn't eaten all day and probably wouldn't eat before leaving in the morning. Before, when she'd traveled with Jake and they'd stayed in hotels, he'd ordered food sent to the room. She didn't think this hotel would accommodate a request like that, leastwise not coming from her. Jake'd paid for everything, too. Well, now she could fling his money back into his face. That'd teach him. She scowled, trying to erase him from her thoughts.

Usually he'd joined her for dinner, encouraging her to eat every bite. She knew she looked half-starved back then. The meager orphanage food often consisted of only two bowls of thin, watery gruel a day. With Jake she'd eaten well, even on the trail. Then Miss Hall had made it her mission to put some weight on Betsy's waiflike frame, and later on Shaun had fed her like she might die of starvation otherwise. She studied herself in the bureau mirror. She had to admit, she looked good wearing the added pounds. Her pants and shirt no longer fell loosely off her body. She was definitely filling out. Did anyone notice besides her?

After pacing the small room for an hour, she sighed heavily, opened the hotel room door, looked up and down the hallway, then tiptoed down the stairs, trying to slip unnoticed into the half-empty café. She sat at a corner table, her back to the entry, unlike any other cowboy would have done, but turned this way she could see the length of the short street from her seat and watch the regular swinging of the saloon doors as whooping miners entered carrying small bags of gold dust. Occasionally one staggered out, already having celebrated himself broke.

After her meal, she decided to check on Moonlight before returning to the room. Fully dark now, no one would pay her much attention. Stanton made her nervous, and she regretted her promise to Shaun.

Back in the room, the ruckus from the street below continued well past midnight, keeping her awake and tossing. At one point she heard whispering outside her door, and she lay paralyzed, heart thumping. Then footsteps trailed down the creaking stairs and she realized she'd not breathed in minutes. If only…no, she wouldn't say it. She'd been about to say if only Jake were here…but she'd never say it. Not ever.

Betsy arose and saddled Moonlight long before dawn, believing herself to be the only person stirring at that hour. It was still warm and sultry, but she hoped that with this early start she'd be up the hill before the heat became too oppressive and burdensome.

"We're off, Moonlight. Let's go home," she crooned quietly as the two started down the dirt wagon road leading out of town. Stopping briefly at the creek, she let the horse take a long drink before proceeding up the rugged, mountainous trail. She remembered camping just a ways down this stream, bathing in a clear pool. It now seemed so long ago that she'd arrived, certain of finding her mother. She never imagined her return would be like this. She felt defeated and more lonely than ever. At least before she'd had hope of seeing her mother again. Now she had no one, except Margaret, and deep down Betsy knew that finding her sister would be a futile task. She'd abandoned her childish ideas of ever finding her the day she buried her mother.

She urged Moonlight on, knowing it best to have the treacherous climb completed before the sun rose too high. She'd let the horse pick its own pace, as long as it didn't run. If the road was still as rough as it had been when she'd ridden down, she estimated it would take two hours to ascend, maybe longer if she let Moonlight rest periodically. She didn't really know if resting was necessary, but she wanted to err on the side of caution when it came to her horse. She'd never owned anything so fine in her life, and she cherished the animal. Hoping that once she got as far as Yarnell she'd feel safe, she already felt immensely better just getting out of Stanton.

Forty-five minutes into the trek she sensed someone trailing her. Several times she heard voices, but she'd been unable to see anyone because of the twisting road and hilly terrain. She saw a switchback just ahead that would give her a good opportunity to look to the road below.

There they were. Two men. Her blood froze as she stared at them, motionless. She recognized the horse, the one in front for certain. Never would she forget the pure-white horse racing past her down the Hassayampa when she'd hid in the bushes. Even the large, black-bearded man looked familiar, but perhaps that was just her imagination. The horse was not her imagination. She'd never seen a pure-white horse before. No gray. No tint. No spot. White. Solid, sheet white. Intuitively, she knew the men had followed her from Stanton and meant her harm. The big, bearded man glanced up and caught her looking at them.

He pulled his rifle from its scabbard, alerting his companion to her presence. Despite her hurry, she seemed to move in slow motion. Kicking

Moonlight with all her strength, she willed the horse to move out. She needed cover.

The first ring of a bullet galvanized Moonlight into the stride Betsy hoped for, and the horse took off up the slope, its hooves scrambling, sliding, and slipping on loose shale and small rocks. Almost bucking in its efforts to lunge forward, the horse finally began to pick up speed. Another bullet zinged by, and Betsy felt a slight stinging sensation in her arm. She bent low over the horse, trying to make herself an even smaller target, worrying lest Moonlight be shot from underneath her. If she could just make it to the next bend where a large rock loomed at the corner of the switchback, she'd be safe.

Slowing Moonlight and sliding off the fear-crazed horse, she grabbed the Henry from its scabbard. Firmly holding the reins of the frightened animal, she grabbed for the box of bullets Shaun had put in the saddlebags, but the horse spun about wildly and she was forced to release the animal. She smacked him firmly on the rump, desperately hoping he would escape unharmed.

Too frightened to clearly think of the imminent danger she faced, she hunkered behind the boulder, using the large rock for protection. She had, at most, a dozen bullets in a cartridge belt Shaun had also forced her to take. Panic began to course through her. The firing ceased, and then she heard intermittent laughter and talking.

Removing her hat, she peeked from behind the rock and saw the men openly advancing on foot, not even attempting to hide, moving in a brazen, cocky manner that suggested complete confidence they would catch their prey. They separated and headed up the hill at opposing angles. It was obvious, even to Betsy in her inexperience, that they planned to come at her from different directions. She leaned against the rock and closed her eyes, her heart pounding in her chest. She'd never felt such fear. If only she could melt into the earth and disappear forever. Momentarily she thought of giving up and begging for mercy, but she quickly abandoned that idea, remembering too well what they'd done to her mother. Clearly envisioning her mother again, face down in the water, she began to pull herself together. She now plainly understood that if she didn't kill these murderers, they'd kill her.

Feeling strangely removed, she methodically loaded the weapon and fit the butt of the rifle snugly against her shoulder. Sighting down the barrel at one of her moving targets, without hesitation she slowly and smoothly squeezed the trigger, trying not to blink.

Never had a blast sounded so loud, and never had one thrown her backwards to the ground before. She sat upright, quickly scrabbling to load the rifle for another shot. That's when a large hand shot out, painfully grabbing her by the arm and yanking her to the rock. Expecting the worst, she resigned herself to the last struggle of her life.

Saving Tom Black

THE return to Prescott proved uneventful and easier than Jake imagined it would. McGraw accompanied the group as far as Tuba City after Jake stopped with his prisoners at the trading post. Neither captive spoke much on the trip, so he largely ignored the two miserably jarred passengers whom he'd securely chained in the back of the wagon. Concerned about the possible appearance of Johnny Geiger, Jake kept a sharp lookout, but never saw a trace of the desperado. There was nothing in it for Geiger anyway at this point, he reasoned. Still, a man didn't always do the reasonable thing.

He'd turn these men over to the authorities at the more securely built and guarded stockade at Fort Whipple, and take a day doing paperwork and making statements. Then, he supposed, he should turn his steps toward finding Betsy's mother so he could be finished with the girl once and for all. Deep inside he understood, although he'd never admit it -- especially to himself -- that his reluctance to find the mother stemmed from the fact that he wasn't really interested in losing track of Betsy. Damn it to hell. He cursed more and more frequently as the miles to Prescott diminished. He wondered when would be a good time to tell Betsy about Margaret. How would he keep her from charging off after her sister? Maybe, he thought, it would be best to keep the news to himself for now.

For three days he received accolades and honors for his arrests, during which time he also silently congratulated himself for not riding by Miss Hall's boarding house. Things changed rapidly, however, when one afternoon he heard a deep, sonorous, southern voice call his name.

"Marshal Silver. Marshal Silver. Please. I'm hopin' to say a few words, with your permission."

Jake recognized Thomas DuBonnet instantly and wondered what the man was doing in

Prescott. "You're a long way from home aren't you, Mr. DuBonnet?"

"The name, suh, is just Thomas Jefferson. DuBonnet is not rightly my name."

"Really?" Amused, Jake feigned surprise.

"Marshal, I have somethin' that's been burnin' a hole in me for some time. I needs t' talk with you."

Jake decided it was not the time for ridicule, and nodded his assent.

"Suh, you 'member that young feller, Tom Black, that was with me back in Albuquerque?"

"Trust me, I'll never forget him," Jake responded, reverting to sarcasm.

"Suh, that warn't no young boy. That be a young girl. Miss Betsy DuBonnet. Suh, I am prepared to face the arm of the law over what transpired if that be necessary, but I'm hopin' you'll see the truth of what I'm sayin'."

"Go on," Jake said, fully enjoying the man's account.

"Suh, I am 'sponsible for that young gal gettin' off that train and takin' off by herself. She be lookin' for her mama, and I come here to find her. I won't never rest 'til I know that young lady be safe agin."

"So, let me understand, Mr. Jefferson, you were aiding and abetting a runaway?"

"Never thought of it like that, Marshal. But if you say so, I'll gladly pay the price if I c'n know for certain that Miss Betsy be safe. I come here lookin' for her but ain't seen hide nor hair of her."

"I assure you, Mr. Jefferson, that Betsy is safe. I escorted her to Prescott myself and know for certain that she's living in the establishment of Miss Virginia Hall. You can go on your way with a clear conscience." Jake turned to leave, but Thomas Jefferson detained him further.

"She's not there, suh."

"And how do you know that, Mr. Jefferson?"

"I watcht all three boardin' houses for a week. Never saw even one glimpse of Miss Betsy. Not one."

"Trust me. She's there," Jake retorted with an impatient, dismissive air. Still Jefferson stood his ground.

"That horse she bought's not in any stable in town, either. Checked 'em all."

Unconcerned, Jake waved the man off and headed for his hotel, but the stack of mail that had been waiting for him loomed, particularly one small, unstamped letter. Returning to his room, he snatched up the little bundle. One bore a postmark from Fort Worth, one originated from Dodge City, a few flyers rounded out the mix, but there also lay a small envelope thick enough to be holding several pieces of stationery, but it bore no stamp. The letter would have to have been dropped off.

Inside he found two pieces of folded paper. Glancing at the signature on the first page, he saw Virginia Hall's name neatly written. Quickly, he scanned the note informing him that Betsy had headed for Wickenburg by herself, but had not returned. Miss Hall had also enclosed a note that Betsy had left for him.

Jake stopped, took a deep breath, and slowly unfolded the other piece of paper. His anger surged before he even began reading.

"Dear Jake, I'm sorry I broke my promise. You taught me well, though, so I'll be fine. I appreciate everything you've done for me, but I can see that you have other responsibilities of far greater importance than looking after me and finding my mother. I don't know what else to say." It was signed, "Your friend always and always, Tom Black."

"Damn it to hell," he muttered through clenched teeth. The letter was dated over a month ago. A sick feeling coursed through him as he grabbed his saddlebag, rifle, extra cartridges, and a blanket. Taking the stairs two at a time, he strode resolutely out the door, stopping only to throw his key on the hotel reception desk. "I don't know when I'll be back. Hold my room," he growled menacingly.

Retrieving his horse from the stable, he refused to think about all the possible catastrophes that could have befallen the girl. Never had he felt more angry and, he had to admit, worried.

Uncharacteristically putting the spurs to his mount, the two departed town leaving a trail of dust. He allowed the animal to fully run, not worried about reserving stamina and strength. Confident that the stage road from Prescott south would be largely free from ambush and desperados, Jake charged on, determined to travel the treacherous, windy road nonstop until he reached Wickenburg. He refused to think about anything but the roadway before him. Least of all he refused to think about Betsy and the possible tragedy that might have befallen her - the same tragedy as had befallen the young girls in Freeman.

Twenty miles down the way his anger began to cool and he reined the horse to a lope. Despite the summer heat, the animal was only slightly damp, but he knew to stop for water as soon as possible. He didn't want to lose the horse, too. He could not shut the undeniable thought from his mind. Now that he was in danger of losing Betsy -- if he hadn't lost her already -- he realized his pretending to be rid of her had to stop. In the rare moments when he could be almost honest with himself, he admitted she'd never once been absent from his thoughts over the past weeks. Seeing Margaret in the canyon had brought back an ache that he'd convinced himself he'd cured, but obviously hadn't. Impossible. Impractical. Damn. He might have to admit that he loved the headstrong, willful, aggravating, charming and beautiful Elizabeth DuBonnet.

The trip from Prescott to Wickenburg, normally a three-day journey at the least, would take him half that time if he continued at this pace and didn't encounter any unforeseen problems. He knew he should stop for a few hours at night to rest and to give the horse a chance to forage, but he didn't want to. His horse needed shoeing, however, something he'd not yet attended to in Prescott, and he didn't want the animal throwing a shoe while on the trail from Yarnell down to Stanton, which he'd heard to be extremely rugged. The odds of that happening in the dark on a rocky road would be much greater than if he waited for daylight.

Exhausted, he resigned himself to stopping for the few short remaining hours of the night before he began the descent to Stanton. Untying his blanket, he settled in and immediately dozed, despite his intentions to remain awake.

The echoing sound of rifle fire awoke him in the early hour before sunrise. The reports came rolling up the hill from the stage road below, echoing off the mountainsides. Quickly gathering his belongings, Jake mounted and began a careful descent. The horse slid on the loose rocks and flagstone, forcing him to keep the animal to a walk. The rifle shots stopped, but now he heard the unmistakable pounding of horse hooves approaching. His trail experience told him only one horse approached, but still he drew his weapon, prepared for the worst.

The grullo raced toward him madly, breathing heavily, its eyes wild with fear. There was no question that the animal was Betsy's Moonlight.

"Whoa, boy. Whoa," Jake spoke firmly as he positioned his horse to slow the oncoming animal so he could grab for its reins. Moonlight, sweating fiercely with sides heaving, stopped, exhausted, and offered no resistance to capture. Foam coated, its nose trickled blood from its frantic race up the hill.

Was Betsy somewhere down the hill, or had someone simply stolen the horse? Dismounting, Jake grabbed his rifle and left both animals to wander while he ran, skidding and sliding, down the hillside. Tossing safety aside, he tore down the steep hill. He figured the horse had run quite a distance to be that worked up, so the shooters wouldn't be close. He estimated that he had at least a half a mile before he'd come upon anyone. He heard no hooves approaching, nor had he heard any more rifle fire.

Coming to a hairpin turn, he slowed, hoping for a vantage point to see down the twisting road. Stooping low and trying to avoid the prickly cactus, he squatted a moment, studying the landscape. His keen eyesight spied movement on the terrain below. At least two men clambered up the steep hillsides, one on each side of the road. They made no attempt to hide, and now he heard their voices drifting toward him. Too noisy to be hunters, caution urged him to watch a minute more before approaching them. Then he saw Betsy hiding behind a boulder at the next switchback down. No mistaking now who the two men were hunting.

Rather than shooting the distant, moving targets, Jake made the decision to get to Betsy before the two men found her. The hillside, blanketed with prickly pear and sharp, jagged rocks, made the going rough, but he felt no pain from the stabbing barbs as he skillfully wove his way down the mountainside undetected. Looking at his shirt he could see he'd be picking thorns for days to come, but he felt no discomfort from the sharp prongs embedded in his clothing and skin. He saw only Betsy, hiding, and now taking a rifle and loading it. He briefly wondered where the hell she'd gotten a rifle, and when the hell had she learned to shoot? Well, nothing she did surprised him anymore, but he *was* surprised at his surprise.

The stalkers, suddenly spotting him, both fired and missed widely. The shots forced Jake to stand in order to move more quickly before they could reload and focus in on his position. Fifty yards and he'd be safe. Leaping down the rugged hillside, he hoped he didn't sprain an ankle, or worse. Twenty yards. He clearly saw the rich, blonde hair gathered at the nape of her neck and her incredibly slender arms expertly holding the rifle as she took aim. Reaching out for her as she fired, he jerked her back and threw her to the ground to keep her behind the safety of the rock. As she scrambled for the rifle, still oblivious to his presence, he roughly grabbed her by the arm, his grip like steel, and spun her around.

Stunned, she momentarily sat motionless before she lunged at his arm, trying to physically attack him. Her helplessness overwhelmed him, despite her valiant efforts. Suddenly their eyes met and, despite his fury, his heart melted when he looked into her large, blue, terrified eyes.

The moment quickly passed, and Jake turned his attention to the business at hand. He knew the positions of the two men and realized he could not get a good shot from behind the boulder.

"How many are there?"

"Only two. I think."

"Stay put. Do you hear me? Don't you *dare* move," he gruffly commanded as he grabbed both rifles and, bent low, headed downhill.

One of the men rose from behind a stubby cactus and took aim. The shot flew wild and wide again. Bending to one knee, Jake raised his rifle, sighted in on the cactus, and fired. The partially obscured shooter fell sideways, but Jake wasn't sure if he'd killed the man or only wounded him, which might still enable the gunman to take more shots. Jake fired again at the heap on the ground and saw it slightly jerk as the bullet struck, but otherwise the body remained motionless.

One more man remained at large, most likely to the right of Jake's present position. Why hadn't he heard, or felt the rifle's report? He urgently needed to find cover in order to locate the second shooter.

Stooping low, he ran toward some larger rocks strewn along the hillside. After throwing himself down among them, he cautiously raised his head to search. A moment later the zing of a bullet hit a nearby rock, sending shards flying.

Jake leaped up and ran. As the man scrambled to reload, Jake brought Betsy's Henry to his shoulder, slid to a stop, aimed, and fired. The man yelled and clutched his left shoulder. Clearly, the rifle's sight was off. He'd have to adjust for that, but meanwhile the wound would slow the man down long enough for Jake to fire off another shot. The man cried for mercy, but there was none in Jake's heart. He quickly reloaded and slowly, methodically, brought the rifle to position, corrected slightly as he sighted down the barrel, and squeezed the trigger. Savage animosity flew with the projectile to its target. The victim fell in a heap, motionless, without a doubt, dead.

Suddenly he heard a pistol fire behind him. Quickly drawing the Colt from its holster, he dropped and rolled, preparing to shoot, fully expecting an attack from a third gunman. Instead, he saw Betsy standing over the first dead outlaw, a small-caliber weapon in her hand. She fired at the prone corpse again, and then again. Even in his anger and bewilderment Jake understood that a grievous wrong had been done to her by the man lying at Betsy's feet. As she riddled the body with bullets, his heart fell at the thought of her suffering at anyone's hands.

A moment later he reached her side and grabbed the weapon, which she surrendered without resistance.

"Betsy, what in hell are you doing?"

She turned, tears streaking her dirt-smeared face. "He killed my mother, Jake. He shot her. He killed her," she sobbed.

Only the prickly cactus barbs embedded in his clothing kept him from sweeping her into his arms.

He let her cry it out, and then to distract her, he said, "Help me get these cactus barbs out." Pulling a few from the front of his shirt, he waited until she moved to help.

Silently, she plucked thorns from his chest, arms, and back. Neither spoke during the procedure, but neither took their eyes from the other for long.

Finally able to move without being pricked, he realized the moment to hold her had long passed.

"Come on. Let's round up the horses. Theirs have got to be on down the road somewhere. We'll retrieve them and get these two up to Yarnell. With luck there'll be an undertaker there."

Betsy silently followed him up the hill. He sensed that she waited for a word of assurance from him, but he didn't oblige her. When he thought of her foolhardy escapade he began to wonder if he could ever trust her, let alone control her. She had a mind of her own, that was certain. Yet, when he thought of the fluffy, powder-puff women he'd known, he had to admit he liked Betsy's spirit far more in comparison. Still, he remained silent, not knowing how to say what he wanted - not knowing what he really wanted to say.

Betsy and Jake's horses had wandered only a short distance from where he'd left them. "I'd tell you to wait here, but you won't. So come on along while I gather the other two horses to pack the bodies out on."

They found the animals tied downhill from the scene of the gunfight. Jake loaded and secured the bodies on the backs of the horses, and the sad little party headed up the stage road.

"We better walk. Your horse just about ran himself to death," Jake commented.

Betsy nodded and reached down to tenderly pat the horse's neck. "I know you're angry, Jake," she said in a quiet, quaking voice. "I can see it in your eyes. In the set of your jaw. Will you ever be able to forgive me?"

"I don't know, Betsy. I want to trust you, but it seems I can't."

"But you can!"

"We'll see." He didn't want to make this easy on her, but he began to take pity on the downcast girl when he remembered about her mother being killed.

"Tell me about...about your mother," he said quietly.

And so she began the incredible tale of finding her mother and her adventures that summer up the Hassayampa River with Shaun Agar. Jake listened in wonder, marveling at the good fortune that once again had befallen her. When she finished the wild story, she wiped her eyes with her dirty sleeve, smudging her face even more.

"I've got money to pay you back, too. Shaun gave me these little bags of coins before I left. I tried to turn him down but he said I'd earned it by keeping him alive and then helping him pan for gold. That was fun." She smiled weakly. "The gold part, I mean."

"I told you, Betsy. You've no need to pay me back. I won't say it again, either."

It took a good hour for Jake to square things with Yarnell's local undertaker. Jake's badge carried enough authority that the man didn't ask questions. No one said a word when the undertaker laid out the bearded man's bullet-riddled body in the wooden coffin, but several locals in attendance glanced about nervously, avoiding eye contact with the marshal. No doubt they all wondered what had actually transpired.

By the time the two desperados had been disposed of, the hour was late. A short distance from Yarnell, Jake and Betsy camped for the night. It almost reminded Jake of old times, except that neither spoke much. He couldn't help but think of the young girl and the miserable job she'd done of trying to pass herself off as a boy. He wanted to laugh out loud at the memory, but kept a stern face instead.

They broke camp early the next morning and rode a long while in silence. Several times Jake started to speak, but stopped himself. He didn't know where or how to begin. Her obvious, pitiful sorrow was eating a hole in him.

"Jake, I missed you," Betsy finally said, abandoning her reserve. "I know you probably don't care, but I thought about you most every day. Sometimes I hated you, but mostly I--I lo--liked you," she stumbled, blushing deeply.

"Well, I thought about you every day, too, Betsy."

"Good thoughts?"

"Mighty good thoughts. To me anyway."

"What? What did you think? Will you tell me?'

"Nope."

"Jake…" she smiled, waiting for him to speak.

Jake stopped and turned to her. Despite Moonlight's height, he still looked down at the beauty before him. "What I'm thinking now is that if you and I are ever gonna get beyond this part of getting to know each other, then only one of us is gonna be able to wear the pants. And that's gotta be me, Betsy. Pure and simple. No negotiating. No arguing. I'm a man. That's what men do. Men wear the pants."

"I understand," she answered simply, looking down at her trousers.

In spite of himself, Jake laughed. "I gotta say, though, you fill out those pants and that shirt darn good. You can't fool anyone anymore calling yourself Tom Black. Those days are long gone. Never saw a Tom Black looking so nice as you do." He winked at her, enjoying her growing smile.

"Jake!" She squirmed a bit in the saddle. "Well, I was wondering if you'd notice. I'm looking more like other women now, don't you think?"

"Much better," he responded, winking again. "Come on. Let's pick up the pace before I say something I'll regret."

Moonbeams

NEITHER Betsy nor Jake seemed inclined to rush back to Prescott. They rode slowly, moseying along, enjoying the warmth, the scenery, but mostly each other's company. At times, Betsy babbled happily and laughed. Other times, her face clouded as she furtively gazed at the man by her side whom she now viewed so differently. Or, perhaps she simply felt different about herself. Certainly, she wasn't the girl she'd been only a few months ago when she'd hidden aboard the outbound train from Topeka. Physically she'd changed, but an even greater change had occurred inside.

While the loss of her mother had been devastating, the change in her had nothing to do with that. She'd thought of nothing these many months but being with Jake Silver. Longing for the feel of his arms wrapped around her and his hard, muscular body pressing close to her, she blushed at these daring thoughts, looking away quickly, fearing he might read her mind. Despite her gaping inexperience in these matters, she knew she was in love and had been from the moment she'd seen him in Albuquerque. Insecurity lurked in her heart, though, and she tormented herself with doubt. Why would he possibly return her affection when he had the pick of any woman in town? She was an orphan. She didn't even know who her father was. Vowing not to let these precious moments with him be dampened by her insecurity, she put on a bold front.

They talked of small things, and Betsy left her feelings and longings unspoken, even though she wanted to venture into that realm of what ifs and maybes. Fearing outright rejection, she kept her tender thoughts to herself.

Dismounting in the shade of a large, leafy cottonwood for a midday break and a bite to eat, they sat silently watching the two horses ripping grass.

"Jake, what's the name of your horse? I don't think I've ever heard you call it by name."

"Well, I call it all kinds of names. Buddy, Pardner, and Sonof-…never mind. I'm not always polite, I suppose."

"I thought you said that naming a horse showed that a person cared."

"Did I say that?"

Betsy laughed. "Yep. You sure did."

He looked away, a bit embarrassed. "You must have me mixed up with one of those other desperados."

"You mean you haven't named your horse?"

"Sure I have. I'm just joshing you," he said. But Betsy wondered in the silence that followed if he struggled to quickly think of a name for the animal.

"Well?"

"Topeka. That's his name. That's where I bought him." In point of fact, he'd bought the horse after a poker game in Dodge, but he boldly continued on with the story, "The name Topeka just seemed so right since that's where you and I first crossed paths."

"That's a great name. That's where I caught the train, you know."

He nodded. "Speaking of trains, you'll never guess who I ran into a few days ago in Prescott."

She thought for some minutes. "I have no idea."

"Your old buddy, Thomas DuBonnet."

"What?"

"Yeah. He's gone back to using his real name now. Came out west to find you. Said he was responsible for you getting off that train and had been worried sick about you since."

"Oh my gosh. That's so, so sweet of him."

"You'll have to let him know you're okay. Probably better if I tell him for you. I think he'll want to see you, though. How do you want to handle that?"

"Is there a problem?" she asked, innocently.

Jake sat a moment and seemed unsure how to proceed. "Betsy, this world is not as…as….Let's just say that this world is complicated. There's hard feelings against black folk by some whites. It might not look good to, say, Miss Hall or others if a black man showed up at the door looking for you."

"Well, I know the truth and so do you and so does Thomas. So who cares what others think?"

"You'll care -- soon enough. Sometimes the truth has nothing to do with it. Tell you what, I'll meet up with him and then have you come by. I'll work it out so you won't be compromised or --" he trailed off. Neither spoke for a few minutes.

"Is it for me, or for yourself, that you think I should be more circumspect?" she finally asked.

"That's a fair question. To be honest, I'm not sure. But think about it. You stole money and ran away; you hid out in a train car alone with a black man; you've spent the summer up river with a strange man who was your mother's lover; you've been hunted by two desperados who would've done more to you than take your money. So, all things considered, I'm not so sure it matters if you're circumspect or not."

"Jake, I don't like what you're saying. It makes me sound, well, bad."

"I know. Good thing I don't see it like that, so you go ahead and make your own decision about Thomas Jefferson. I'll stand by whatever you decide." He smiled at her. "If we want to get to Prescott tomorrow, we best mount up and head off." He took her hand, pulling her up from the grassy resting spot.

She studied him while he held Moonlight's reins. She noticed that he stood closer to her than needed, and their eyes continually met. Suddenly, he wrapped his arm about her and drew her to him. The tender kiss that followed lingered, and neither of them wanted to stop. Finally, he pulled slightly away and lifted her to the saddle.

Their return to Prescott did not go unnoticed. "So much for being circumspect," Betsy joked.

Virginia Hall gave Betsy a good scolding and then hugged her, all the while weeping in relief. The older woman looked from one to the other with knowing eyes. Clearly, she saw the bloom of love on their faces.

"Well, young lady, you're going to have to tell me all about your latest adventures. It just makes my heart race to think of what you must have been through all this time."

Turning to Jake Silver, she said, "Marshal, I'm thankful for Betsy's safe return. You're welcome in this house any time."

As the weeks passed it became apparent to many that Elizabeth DuBonnet had become Marshal Silver's girl. Often together, they attended several civic functions. Despite the male attention she garnered, it was obvious that she had eyes only for the man by her side.

Thomas Jefferson, with Miss Hall's approval, called upon Betsy at the boarding house. Miss Hall ushered the humble man into the parlor, then to Betsy's surprise left the room, quietly closing the glass-paned door behind her.

"Miss Betsy – okay to call you Miss Betsy these days? Not Tom Black no more?"

Both laughed, and she invited him to sit.

"How are you doing, Thomas? Jake told me you came to save me. I can't tell you how touched I am by that."

"Miss Betsy, I'm the happiest man alive that you be alive and well. It's a miracle. I prayed for a miracle. I said, Oh, Lawd, grant me a miracle and take care o' dat girl. Looks like He did." Thomas smiled proudly.

"Tell me what happened after we parted, Thomas."

"Not a long story. Guess you could say I had a run of bad conscience. Got me some money I'd set aside earlier in my younger years and promised myself I wouldn't stop lookin' for you until I found you. Pretty simple."

"What're you going to do now? Do you have work?"

"I got a bit o' money. I'm bidin' my time. I'll find somethin' right soon. Don't you worry none."

"Well, I'll give you a reference if you wish. I know Marshal Silver will, too. Please, let me help you if I can."

"That's right generous, Miss Betsy. I thank you. Say, I want to tell you how very sorry I am about your mama. I heard talk that she been killed. Right sorry about your loss."

"Thank you, Thomas."

The two chatted for a few more minutes before Thomas stood to leave.

"What a lovely man," commented Miss Hall as she watched Jefferson exit the gate and walk away toward town.

"Yes. He was very kind to me. And then he came all the way out here to find me. I wish there was a way that I could repay him."

"It seems everyone wants to save that darned Tom Black," Virginia teased. "You'd think that young man could keep out of trouble. Personally, I think it's one of the most exciting tales I've ever heard."

Virginia helped Betsy open a bank account, both women shocked at how much money the leather pouches Shaun Agar gave her contained. The smaller of the two held over four hundred dollars in coin, while the large carried two thousand. Betsy's first act was to send forty-four dollars plus interest to the orphanage, an act that evoked a look of puzzlement from the bank's manager. When she didn't offer an explanation, no further questions were asked.

***

Weeks quickly passed, and September's heat rapidly faded to cool, crisp mornings followed by even colder evenings. Jake became a regular dinner guest at the Virginia Hall House and amused the residents with tales of Kansas and cattle drives. Often he stayed late, and more and more frequently he and Betsy began to talk about the what ifs and the maybes of their relationship. Their courtship, romantic and cozy, made it difficult for the two to remain virtuous. Near impossible for Jake. On his forays from Prescott he thought only of the winsome girl he hoped was still waiting, and she, in his absence, dreamed of nothing but his return. Twice his distraction came close to costing him his life. Disgusted by his lovesick state, he finally made up his mind that things had to change if he was going to live long enough to become her husband. On the trail he had to be all business, pure and simple. But his craving for her had to be satisfied sooner than later. Things needed to change.

But the change that came was not what either anticipated. A courier hand delivered Betsy a letter from a local solicitor one morning in late fall, requesting her presence at a private hearing the following day. Certain that the summons was the result of the theft she'd committed months earlier, she immediately sought Jake's protection, praying he could keep her from prison. Despite his reassurances that no one had ever been sent to jail for forty-four dollars, Betsy still spent a sleepless night until Miss Hall invited her to share a short brandy, "just between us girls." Quickly the two began giggling quietly, soon laughing loudly, to the consternation of the other boarders.

Mr. Arnold met Betsy at the appointed hour. He seemed surprised that Jake Silver and Virginia Hall accompanied her. He looked nervously from one to the other, his small, pale blue eyes blinking rapidly as though trying to decide if their attendance was correct protocol. Despite the chilly temperatures, the heavyset, sweating man eventually plopped into a swivel chair, tugging on the tight collar binding his throat, his wispy white hair plastered to his pasty scalp.

"Miss DuBonnet, are you at all familiar with a Shaun Agar?"

Betsy glanced toward Jake. "Yes. I know Mr. Agar."

"Are you aware that you are his sole beneficiary?"

"No," Betsy responded, her face growing pale.

"I regret to inform you, Miss DuBonnet, that Mr. Agar has passed away. Due to an accident, I believe is what I read."

"Oh no! How horrible! What happened?"

"The cause of the accident is not in my information, but he has been interred in a graveyard in Wickenburg, as I understand it. I sympathize with your loss, Miss DuBonnet. However, it seems that Mr. Agar has left you a wealthy young woman. A very wealthy young woman, indeed." The attorney flipped through the papers before him.

"There must be a mistake. Are you sure it's not my mother named in the Will? Marie DuBonnet?"

"No. Quite clearly, Mr. Agar's last will and testament identifies one Elizabeth DuBonnet, daughter of the late Marie DuBonnet and Sir Alexander Harrington of Georgia, as his sole heir."

Betsy's mind reeled. "Alexander Harrington is my father?"

"Apparently so. However, his presence is not needed under these circumstances since you are, it says here, eighteen as of a month ago."

"Oh, my!"

"Yes, dear, it's true. Mr. Shaun Agar has left his entire fortune to you, which includes fifty thousand dollars in gold and controlling interest in at least a dozen mines."

Opposite Mr. Arnold, the three sat silent and stunned, no one speaking for a full thirty seconds.

"I, I don't know what to say. I -- I'm speechless."

"It's always quite a shock when one comes into a large sum of money. My advice is to invest it wisely and keep mum about your good fortune. I would, of course, be happy to offer my services to you."

"What do I need to do?"

"Sign here acknowledging that you have been duly informed of this matter and tell me where you wish the money and deeds sent."

***

Throughout the proceeding, Jake physically withdrew. Although happy for Betsy's good fortune, he held a bad feeling that now things between them would inevitably change. *He* wanted to be the source of her financial support. He wanted to take care of her. Now, because of her newly acquired wealth, perhaps she wouldn't need him at all anymore. During the proceeding, she'd looked at him questioningly. She'd even sought his hand to hold, which surprised him.

Leaving Mr. Arnold's office, none of the three spoke. Betsy seemed to be in a state of shock. Virginia readily saw that the two needed time alone and excused herself, promising to meet them later for a celebratory lunch.

"Jake, what are you thinking?"

"This is, well, it's great, Betsy. Congratulations. You must be very happy."

"This isn't what I want, Jake. I don't want things to change between us and you seem troubled. This money means nothing to me. I only want our happiness. The money will help make us happy." Excited, she added, "You can quit being a lawman and stay home!"

"So I can be your butler? Not gonna happen, Betsy. A man takes care of his woman, not the other way around. Leastwise, not in any house I care to live in."

"I'll, I'll give the money away then," she said, both knowing even as she spoke that it would never happen.

"Do with it what you will, Betsy. It's your money. From Shaun." He paused a moment, but was unable to stop himself from adding in an unmistakable, insinuating tone, "How close were you two, anyway?"

Even before he finished the sentence he regretted his lapse into sarcasm and innuendo.

"How dare you say something like that to me," she hissed, bursting into tears.

"I'm sorry, Betsy. That was uncalled for. I just don't know where this is gonna go now that you're the richest woman in Prescott, maybe in the whole West."

"Nothing has to change, Jake!"

"It already has. You're already wanting me to quit work and be a houseboy. I'm a lawman, Betsy. That'll never change. Never. Do you hear me?"

"Jake, we can travel. Think of that! We can go to Europe, or South America. We can buy a beautiful ranch..." She trailed off, a faraway look in her eyes. "Jake, I can buy Ruth Jeffries' magnificent forty-acre parcel with the beautiful log home. She had it up for sale a while back. It's the embodiment of my dream home --"

"Tell you what," Jake cut her off. "You give all this some thought. We'll talk later." There'd really be nothing left to say. He had no doubt that Betsy's head would be turned with all the money. He couldn't blame her. She'd grown up with nothing, and now she'd just been given everything. She'd received more from Shaun Agar than he'd ever be able to give her in ten lifetimes, that was certain. He abruptly brushed past her, leaving her standing alone in the vestibule of the small courthouse.

He spent two frustrating weeks on the trail, riding mindlessly, feeling the cold of December creep into his bones. He'd been so happy -- how was it possible things had turned so dismal? As the temperature fell, his feelings for Betsy began to cool and harden. Sometimes he congratulated himself on escaping. At other moments he deeply regretted his loss. More than a few times he visited with saloon hostesses in an effort to crush her in his mind, but his pleasure with bar whores quickly waned. He wanted Betsy. As the days wore on, his annoyance grew.

A bitter winter kept him prisoner in Prescott. Heavy snow accumulation made the dark pine forests of the high country completely inaccessible. During that time he read voluminously, trying to lose himself in the lives of others. He paced the small hotel room, cleaned his weapons until they liked to drip with oil, and groomed his horse until the stable hand teased him about brushing the animal hairless. Finally, unable to stand the confines of town, he journeyed the short distance south to Wickenburg.

One day's ride from Prescott the snow lay only in patches; another half day and the ground was clear. The cold weather continued, but the dry weather allowed him to ride Topeka in ease. It felt good to ride wildly, and the horse enjoyed the cool, brisk air, eagerly snorting for a good run.

As the days passed, a growing anger replaced his sense of loss. He realized he'd been a fool for wasting time over the matter. Women were only women, and there were lots of them. The hell with her. She'd been nothing but trouble from the get-go.

Miners and their squabbles filled the rowdy little town of Wickenburg. Four times Jake broke up barroom brawls, and on one occasion he beat a man senseless. Once he'd started, his slow-burning anger had flared to an uncontrollable rage. After this occasion, townspeople gave him a wide berth and plenty of respect.

He seldom thought of Betsy, relieved now to be rid of her. Yet, despite his liberation, he found himself investigating Shaun Agar. What he learned pretty much coincided with what Betsy'd told him. He found out Agar had a reputation as an honest, hard-working man and had made Betsy his sole beneficiary after she'd left to return to Prescott. Every person vouched for Agar. Men all wanted to tell the tale of Agar beating John Casey to death to save Marie. They spoke of him as a local hero.

Jake roamed clear to Phoenix where he enjoyed warmer weather for a month, but inevitably he knew he had to return to Prescott if he wanted to keep his job. Unfortunately, his first moments in town found him face to face with Virginia Hall, the woman smiling graciously but staring daggers.

"Marshal Silver! What a pleasant surprise! I'm so glad to see you," Virginia gushed, taking his hand and holding it a moment, a dangerous glint appearing in her eyes.

"Miss Hall. Hello," he began, not certain what he was expected to say.

"Jacob, I'm very disappointed in you." The woman turned like a chameleon. "I don't know what the trouble is between you and Betsy, but she has suffered terribly because of your absence."

"Sorry, ma'am. Don't know why she'd suffer with all that money. Seems pretty lame," he bristled.

"Don't ma'am me, Marshal Silver. You ought to be ashamed. Betsy has sat in that large house she bought completely isolated and alone. If it weren't for Mr. Jefferson taking care of the place I'd be worried sick about her. He reports to me faithfully, you know."

"Pity. I figured she'd have a passel of suitors by now."

"Indeed, and she would, but she'll have none of it. It's shameful, all of this."

He stood, chastised yet flustered. Maybe to some it did seem childish, but to him it was about his manhood.

"I'll call upon her, Miss Hall," he said, not intending to do anything of the sort.

"Marshal Silver, I see clearly that you are a man of good judgment. She purchased the Jeffries place, you know."

"No ma'am, I didn't know."

"Yes, it's --"

"I know where it is, Miss Hall. I reckon I been by there plenty times. Before Betsy bought it. Beautiful place. It ought to suit her just fine."

"Yes, it was Betsy's fondest dream until this misunderstanding arose, but she's still determined to make a working ranch out of it, with Mr. Jefferson's help."

"Good for her," he said flatly.

"Thank you, Marshal. I shan't keep you any longer. Good day." With that Virginia Hall scooped up her skirts and swooped out the door, a silly, conspiratorial grin on her flushed face.

In a pig's eye would he go calling upon her, he vowed.

The Jeffries home, or what had once been the Jeffries home, sat on forty acres slightly west of town in pine country, with snowy peaks standing guard over the pristine homestead.

In spite of everything, he felt drawn toward it by a magnetic force stronger than he could resist. As Topeka ambled up the long drive, he could see Thomas Jefferson putting new rails on a portion of the corral where a snow-laden tree had fallen during the winter.

"Mornin', suh. Good to see you. I was wonderin' when you'd come by."

"Good to see you again, too, Thomas."

"I'll take yo' horse, suh. Go right on up. I think Miss Betsy's gonna be right happy to see you. Ain't seen her smile but one time all this long, cold winter. That bein' when the baby calf was born last week," he added by way of explanation.

Disgusted that he'd given in to coming here, Jake sauntered up to the house, wondering what he'd possibly say to Betsy when he saw her. Well, he'd tell her about her sister; that was a good enough reason for a visit. She had money now – she could hire a Pinkerton detective to retrieve Margaret from the canyon. He stamped his feet on the wide wooden porch in an effort to remove snow and mud, and looked out over the beautiful vista. Virginia Hall had been right. Betsy had it all – mountain views, pastures, even a stream. He gazed out over the cleared fields, a handful of cows and horses roaming freely, including Moonlight who bucked and snorted in the spring air. The place reminded him a bit of the ranch he'd grown up on in Fort Worth. He watched the grullo kick up his heels, and admired the fine-looking animal.

Reluctantly, he turned to knock, and there she stood. "Betsy," was all he said as she slowly approached. Unexpectedly, he pulled her roughly into his arms and held her tightly.

She stood on her toes, attempting to kiss his face, then weeping and burying her face in his wool coat as they stood in the crisp spring air.

"Hey, you," he whispered, "I see you found a moonbeam."

"Hey yourself," she responded. "I'm holding one now." She smiled, stoically wiping away her tears.

Suddenly, he swept her up into his arms and carried her into the house, their lips meeting in a deeply anticipated, passionate kiss. She looked and felt far more irresistible than he remembered. He would wait no more.

Book II of the Jake Silver Adventures:

Apache

When would he kill her?

For a month Nantan Lupan watched her from the bolder- strewn hillside. Sometimes he hid all day among the large rocks observing the woman's fruitless efforts to restore the poorly constructed, one-room adobe structure. Even before her pathetic attempts to rebuild her *casa*, she'd spent three days digging a shallow grave in the rock-hard earth, then tugging the bloated, rapidly rotting corpse of the dead man toward the pitiful hole. With great effort, she'd finally managed to roll the body into the pit and cover it with sand and rocks. She'd wasted no tears on the corpse, and soon turned her full attention to the half-destroyed house.

She puzzled him. Most white women departed immediately after an attack, often leaving their husbands and family to rot in the hot sun, but this one had stubbornly stayed. Her grit pleased him. He dared not tell his brother warriors why he'd spared her life when they'd questioned him. They would have called him a woman if he'd spoken the truth. But it'd been her eyes – those eyes the color of the great pine needle – the color of the ocotillo's leaf that had saved her.

He'd looked into those ocotillo-green eyes twice and would never forget them. The first time had been at the Warwick Trading Post. Three women alighted from the stagecoach many days ago– all three having journeyed west, he'd heard, to serve as wives. Unlike the other two who looked tired and worn, heavy with the smell of white man's use, this one stood erect, a determined chin and straight back marking her the daughter of a military man, or even a chief's wife, were she Indian.

She'd looked directly at him, her eyes momentarily locking with his. He'd detected no flash of disdain or loathing. No fear. White women always avoided eye contact with Indians, turning their heads and looking away in fright and disgust. It had been he who'd shown discomfort, and he'd grown angry that she caused him this discomfort and that he'd shown weakness by looking away first.

He'd looked into those eyes a second time the night of the massacre. He'd ridden with Goso and three other Apaches to avenge the insult and beating of Goso's brother, Istee, by a cluster of white men at the Trading Post. Istee had been warned to avoid the taunts of the white men, but his youth made him respond rashly. The men had taken a knife to the Istee's hair, then savagely bludgeoned the young boy in the head and groin with their rifle butts. In revenge, the small Apache band massacred five settlers, among them the pig of a white man who'd laid claim to the woman with the ocotillo eyes. His brothers would have killed her also had he not grabbed her first, at once surprised by the softness of her skin, the pools of sorrow in her eyes.

She'd stood still and calm as the air before a great storm when the small band attacked; but the hateful man, his voice screeching in fury, toppled heavily when struck. She'd watched the melee as Nantan Lupan's marauders partially destroyed the structure, and once again he'd looked into those cactus-colored eyes when he'd roughly pulled her from under the falling porch roof and thrown her to the ground. She'd uttered no sound while waiting for the fatal thrust as he knelt over her, his knife at her throat. When she'd bravely clasped his wrist, stilling the knife, he'd shoved her aside, then strode to his horse, signaling to the others.

"You go. Go now," he'd commanded her as he mounted his pony. But she'd not gone, even though he'd left the dead man's horse. Now he felt drawn to watch every move the puzzling white woman made.

His fellow Apache brothers didn't understand his fascination with the woman and often teased him about her. He ignored their ribbing, hoping that doing so would cause them to stop. But what they said held truth.

They numbered five, the last remaining braves of Geronimo's tribe of the Bedonkohe Apaches. Goso and his brother Istee, along with Kenoi, had been expelled from Geronimo's village long before, but he and Cavallo had joined up with the other three only when Geronimo had acquiesced and entered into the white man's craftily spun web of tongue-splitting lies. Now the small band of warriors traveled only at night, camping in well hidden, secluded spots in an effort to avoid the American troops and the Mexican soldiers. For the most part, the group avoided confrontation with whites. Even those at the Trading Post where the band often exchanged their meager goods for inferior necessities, begrudgingly tolerated the renegade survivors.

Fascinated by the white woman who showed no fear, Nantan Lupan, known as Grey Wolf to the white man, grew increasingly obsessed. From the start he'd taken dangerous chances to see her, even sneaking to the back of the hateful white man's *casa* the first night the woman arrived. Disgusted, he'd watched the vile man mount her. Quick and brutal, the man had finished in but a moment. He'd then risen from the prostrate woman, leaving her alone where she lay with her hands covering her face. The filthy man ignored her for some time, then returned to savagely take her again. Unable to perform, he angrily issued commands, jerking her from the cot.

He'd watched the proceedings from the shadow cast by the crumbling building. He didn't know all the ways of the white man, but he knew that no Apache would approach his woman in such a manner. He wondered how this woman, unlike any white woman he'd ever seen, came to be with such a man. White men remained inexplicable. Perhaps they all took their women that way. If so, no wonder women left their corpses to rot.

Since the killing, Nantan Lupan had twice more stood at the woman's window, watching her sleep. On one visit he'd even entered the house. She'd stirred uneasily as he'd lightly fingered her long, soft, sand-colored hair, but she didn't awaken. Noiselessly, he left a large chunk of dried meat on the table. He did not have food to spare, but he would not have her starve, nor would he have her leave.

FORTHCOMING LARGE PRINT BOOKS

Jere D. James, *Apache*, Book II of the Jake Silver Adventure Series. Historical Fiction.

Jere D. James, *Canyon of Death*, Book III of the Jake Silver Adventure Series. Fiction.

Rusty Richards, *Casey Tibbs – Born to Ride*. Biography.

Becky Coffield. *Life Was A Cabaret: A Tale of Two Fools, A Boat, and a Big-A** Ocean.* Award-winning. Humorous/Travel/Nonfiction. 2006.

TITLES BY MOONLIGHT MESA ASSOCIATES, INC:

Standard Print and Kindle Editions

Death in the Desert. Suspense. R.L. Coffield . 2009. ISBN 978-0-9774593-3-9 (Book III of the Ben Thomas Series)

Northern Escape. Award-winning Suspense. R.L. Coffield. 2006/2009 Reissue. ISBN 978-0-9774593-4-6 (Book I of the Ben Thomas Series)

Northern Conspiracy. Mystery. R.L. Coffield. 2011. ISBN 978-0-9827585-5-7 (Book II of the Ben Thomas Series)

Saving Tom Black. Western. Jere D. James. 2009. ISBN 978-0-9774593-5-3

Apache. Western. Jere D. James, 2010. ISBN 978-0-9774593-7-7.

Canyon of Death. Jere D. James. 2011 ISBN: 978-0-9827585-4-0

Casey Tibbs – Born to Ride. Rusty Richards.
Biography. 2010.
ISBN: 978-0-9827585-0-2 (Paperback)
978-0-9774593-9-1 (Hardbound)

The Littlest Wrangler. J.R. Sanders. 2010.
ISBN 978-0-9774593-8-4.

Life Was a Cabaret: A Tale of Two Fools, A Boat, and a Big-A** Ocean. Award-winning Nonfiction. 2006.
ISBN: 978-0-9774593-0-8

orders@moonlightmesaassociates.com

www.ingramcontent.com/pod-product-compliance
Lightning Source LLC
Chambersburg PA
CBHW032233010726
47494CB00002B/478

9 780982 758564